STOP RAPING SALLY

JIM IVY

iUniverse, Inc.
Bloomington

Stop Raping Sally

This is a work of fiction. All of the characters, names, incidents, organizations, and dialogue in this novel are either the products of the author's imagination or are used fictitiously.

iUniverse books may be ordered through booksellers or by contacting:

iUniverse
1663 Liberty Drive
Bloomington, IN 47403
www.iuniverse.com
1-800-Authors (1-800-288-4677)

Because of the dynamic nature of the Internet, any web addresses or links contained in this book may have changed since publication and may no longer be valid. The views expressed in this work are solely those of the author and do not necessarily reflect the views of the publisher, and the publisher hereby disclaims any responsibility for them.

Any people depicted in stock imagery provided by Thinkstock are models, and such images are being used for illustrative purposes only.

Certain stock imagery © Thinkstock.

ISBN: 978-1-4620-4592-1 (sc)
ISBN: 978-1-4620-4593-8 (hc)
ISBN: 978-1-4620-4591-4 (ebk)

Printed in the United States of America

iUniverse rev. date: 11/12/2011

CHAPTER 1

It was Friday, 10:35 p.m. as Maggie had dropped her daughter off at mother's night out a new program at her church designed for young couples or young mothers to have a social life. Once a month, the hours were from seven till midnight. She only had about an hour and a half to find her sister, who never missed ladies night at the caravan nightclub. Maggie had been trying desperately to reach her sister for the past hour, as Maggie walked hurriedly into the nightclub. Searching through the crowd immediately she spotted her sister standing at the bar talking with a distinguished looking older man with a beer in his hand. Maggie's sister was named Andrea walking up behind her. Maggie touched her on the shoulder and Andrea turned around, spilling her drink. She shouted, hey sister, what are you doing here? She then hugged Maggie. With a worried look of desperation and tears welling up inside before Maggie could utter a word. Suddenly, a man—six foot two, scruffy-looking, and wearing a trench coat—burst into the bar, shouting, "Maggie Jackson!" at the top of his voice.

A handsome woman turned around.

The disturbed man glared at Maggie. Then he pulled an Uzi out from under his coat and opened fire in the vicinity of the woman, hitting her several times. People ran everywhere. When the clip was empty, the deranged man started to reload.

Suddenly an off-duty police officer dove under a pool table, pulled her weapon, and emptied her gun into the man. The shooter fell like a sack of potatoes.

The officer climbed out from under the pool table. Very shaken over what had just happened, she nevertheless took charge of the situation, holding her badge up high so everyone could see and shouting, "I am Officer Jamie Bell. Now everybody remain calm!"

About five foot eight, Jamie was twenty-eight years old, had long brown hair and blue eyes, and was standing at her full height when she reached for her radio. Jamie radioed, "Officer needs assistance and ambulance at The Caravan night club. The address is 1215 South Peoria Ave. We have multiple victims," she concluded, her voice starting to quiver.

Jamie started to assess how many people had been hit by the madman's gunfire. Counting as many as nine people hit, she tried to arrange the victims and perform whatever triage she could to communicate to the emergency responders a full report and direct them to the most severe injuries when they arrived. Two bartenders and four waitresses tried to help her.

When the police arrived, Captain Richard Jackson yelled out asking what had happened! The captain stood tall at six foot three. Thirty-eight years old, well built, and very handsome, he carried himself with tremendous confidence and authority.

The young policewomen stood up from helping some of the wounded. She told him what had happened and how she'd handled the situation. The crowd cheered for her, and several of the patrons came to the captain and praised the young woman for her heroism.

The captain asked, "What is your name, officer?"

She said, "Jamie, Captain, Officer Jamie Bell."

Another officer yelled across the room, "Captain, get over here!" The officer was holding the hand of a woman as she lay on the floor. She was critically wounded.

The captain came over and saw the woman in blood-soaked clothing. She looked as if she was barely alive.

The captain shouted, "Maggie," and knelt by her side. He lifted her head up and brushed the hair out of her face.

"She's his wife," the other officer whispered.

The woman opened her eyes and looked at her husband. Maggie tried to speak, gasping for air. Her husband whispered into her ear. She reached for him, poking him in the eye. He pulled back and then wiped his eyes.

A moment later, she was gone, and a few of the police officers tried to console the captain. He appeared to be very distraught, and Jamie felt shaken as she stood and watched her police captain grieve for his wife. Watching his wife die made Jamie sick to her stomach. She quickly ran to the bathroom and vomited in a trashcan.

Three other women had died also; one of the victims was Maggie's sister.

The captain stood up and instructed the officers, "Get all the statements from the witnesses and report back to me."

After the captain had left the bar, the other officers worked the room, interviewing everyone they could, including Jamie.

After about an hour, Jamie asked if she could go home. The officers told her to go home and report back in the morning. Sitting inside her car in the parking lot, the emotion of the night had finally gotten to Jamie as she sobbed uncontrollably into her folded arms on her steering wheel. That was the first time she had ever fired her weapon at anyone, much less killed someone.

She started her car and headed home. Three blocks from her house, she stopped at a stop sign. Glancing over at the sign, she noticed something written on it that she couldn't quite make out. She pulled closer. "Stop Raping Sally," the words said. *How awful,* she thought. *Who would write something like that?* Words had been scrawled over the next sign as well. "You can stop him," the sign proclaimed.

Jamie drove to the last stop sign she'd reach before arriving at home. Just like on the other signs, a hand-painted message with each letter running sickly down the sign said, "Stop and listen." She was really puzzled. She felt like it was some sort of message, but to whom?

As she drove into her driveway, she kept thinking about the stop signs. They really bothered her. She tried to put them out of her mind. She felt like she needed to talk to someone. Jamie's mother had passed away when she was eleven years old; though she'd had a falling out with her father several years ago, he'd recently reached out to her. A month ago, Jamie's brother was an Olympic champion wrestler; the two of them had never been very close.

So for the first time in a long time, she called her father. The phone rang four times before Jamie's father answered. From his voice, it was clear that he had just woken up; it was 1:30 in the morning after all.

"Dad, it's me. I needed to talk to someone," Jamie said, her lips quivering. When she added, "I killed a man tonight," she started to cry.

Her father tried to console her, although sympathy was never one of his best traits. He was always very tough on both of his children, especially Jamie's brother. He tried to convince Jamie to move back home. She could be a policewoman there in her hometown.

Jamie answered like she always did—she had told him when she left that she wanted to make it without being under her brother's shadow. She wanted no favoritism. She wanted to do it on her own.

"I know," her dad said, "but you're five hundred miles away. Are you ever going to move back home?"

"Someday I will," Jamie answered, "but not until I've made it here as a detective. That's what I want."

They talked a few minutes more. Jamie told him what had happened and why she was so upset. He gave her his standard speech about being tough, telling her to either suck it up or quit! Jamie thought that was exactly what she wanted to hear, somewhere in the back of her mind. Jamie was quite aware that the speech was exactly why she had called her father. Jamie knew that they would both say, "I love you" before hanging up and that she would call him later next week.

Jamie went into her house, took a shower, and went to bed. She slept, and she didn't dream about what had happened at the nightclub. She dreamed about the stop signs and their meaning instead.

CHAPTER 2

The next morning, she felt very tired. She had tossed and turned all night, but all she could remember about the dreams were the stop signs. *This is crazy,* she thought. *I killed a man last night, and all I can think about are three stop signs that some kid probably wrote on as a joke.*

She opened her refrigerator, grabbed a can of Diet Coke, and took a big drink. After some toast and jelly, she got dressed, locked her door, and headed for the police station. When she came to the first stop sign, she saw that nothing had been written on the side that faced her. As she pulled past it, she focused on her rearview mirror so she could examine the other side. Nothing was written across the sign. Jamie rubbed her eyes to make sure they were clearly focused. She continued on to the next stop sign, pulled past it, and looked out her window. Nothing was on that sign either. When she got to the third stop sign, she got out of her car, walked out to the sign, and looked on the other side. Nothing was there.

I dreamed the whole stupid thing, she thought. *Maybe I was trying to block out the shooting.*

Convincing herself that must have been what happened, she got back into her car and drove to work. When she walked into the station, all of the police officers stood up and clapped. Several shook her hand. One of the police officers handed her a note. It said the police captain was waiting for her in his office and that she was to report there immediately.

Jamie was now in his office. He told her to sit down, which she did. He was reading her file to himself. "It says here your brother was a two-time Olympic champion and that you also wrestled. You studied karate. You were a top marksman on the gun range, and you finished second in your class at the police academy. Interesting."

He finally said, "I see here that you want to be a detective."

"Very much, sir, very much!" she answered.

"You think you can pass the test?"

She nodded and said, "Yes."

"Here is the situation. We have had three detectives transfer. So we are really shorthanded, and the city council would like us to promote a woman, so the mayor has given me special permission to skip the normal procedure and promote someone immediately. If you pass the test, and the psychiatrist clears you, this can happen today.

"There is one test at three o'clock today. I'm going to let you take it. If you pass you still will have to meet with the psychiatrists three times in the next two weeks. I know this is happening really fast. But if I didn't think you were up to the task, I wouldn't do it. Your first case, we will be able to put this case behind us."

Jamie looked a little confused and said, "What case?"

He answered, "The case that was opened last night when a mad gunman opened fire on a crowded bar. That would look good on your résumé, solving your first case."

Jamie just nodded and said, "Okay."

"Not everyone gets a private test," the chief said. "This is a reward for doing a good job. Now, don't let me down. You have some studying to do before three o'clock, so take the rest of the day to study and be back here at two thirty. That will be all."

Thanking him, Jamie left his office and went downstairs to the police study room. After a couple of hours of study, Jamie went to lunch.

On her way, she glanced at the first stop sign. "Stop Raping Sally" it said again. It was like the stop sign by her house. Staring at the sign, she nearly rear-ended another driver. She pulled over, walked up to the sign, and touched it with her hand. She had already convinced herself the writing on the signs had been a dream. Maybe it was this sign she had seen and it had gotten into her subconscious somehow.

She drove to one of her favorite eating spots. She could order her food and study quietly. After an hour, she went back to her car. She could see that a local restaurant had put flyers under every car's windshield wipers. She picked the flyer up and read it. Just as she was about to throw it away, she noticed that something was written by hand on the back side of the flyer.

"Stop Raping Sally," it said.

Jamie was so startled she dropped the flyer immediately. Then she ran to the next car and pulled the flyer off of its windshield. She turned it over. There was nothing. She went to the next three cars and did the same exact thing. Nothing was written on any of their flyers.

Someone is playing a trick on me, she decided. *That has to be it. I'm a young police officer about to become a detective. This must be some kind of prank. I bet whoever's behind this is having some kind of laugh back at the police station at my expense. I'll just pretend nothing has happened.*

She drove back to the station. She only had an hour before the test. She knocked on the police captain's door.

"Come in," he said. "Are you ready for the test?"

She nodded her head and said, "Yes." Jamie started out the door and then paused and turned around, facing the captain. "Captain, do you know of anyone who might be playing a prank on me?"

He answered that he wasn't aware of any.

"Three separate occasions I have come across the same handwritten message—twice on a stop sign and once on a restaurant flyer. Each time, the message says 'Stop Raping Sally.'"

The captain looked puzzled. He leaned back in his chair, put his hands behind his head, and said, "That's weird. Do you think someone is doing this to you? Or is it just a coincidence?"

Jamie just shook her head and said, "I don't know what to think."

At that instant, the captain's phone rang. He answered, nodding his head back and forth. He hung up the phone and said, "They're ready for you."

Jamie went upstairs to the testing room.

The test took about an hour and a half. It had been a pretty grueling test, but she felt she had done well. It was now six o'clock, and she was still waiting for the results.

Finally they came. The captain called her into his office. "Congratulations, Detective," he said, shaking her hand. He then handed her a photo of the man who had shot up the bar and asked her to find out what she could and report back to him. "Remember, make your report complete and thorough. Be sure to question all the people at the bar that you can find and, remember, you're a police detective now. Sometimes these cases aren't what they seem. Sometimes there's no reason for people's crazy behavior at all. He was probably just a nut with a gun and nothing more."

Jamie smiled and left the captain's office. Several other officers congratulated her as she left the station.

On the way home she stopped at the Caravan, the nightclub where the shooting happened. Inside, she asked for the manager. When he came out, she took out her pad and pencil and asked him several questions about the previous night. He answered them the best he could. Jamie then asked him which waitresses were on duty. He pointed out Jill and Sandy and said the others hadn't showed up for work yet. Jamie thanked him and went over to the women.

Jill said, "Hey! You're that cop from last night. You sure stopped that asshole with a gun last night."

Jamie replied, "It's not something I'm proud of. I just reacted. I'm sorry he died."

Sandy said, "I'm not. If you hadn't killed him, he probably would have killed more people."

Jamie just nodded her head and said, "I have a few questions about last night. Have either of you ever seen that guy before?"

They both shook their heads no.

"Was there anything odd or different you noticed last night—anything, anything at all?"

"Well," Jill replied, "I thought that was strange when that woman lunged at that man and poked him in the eye."

Sandy said, "She wasn't lunging for him. She was reaching for him. That was her husband, dummy," Jill retorted, "From my angle," she said while shaking her head in disagreement, "it looked like she was going after him, if you know what I mean." Then Sandy said while rolling her eyes, "You're so stupid. You think everything has a hidden meaning. It was an accident. She was dying. Not everything is a big conspiracy. You watch way too much TV."

As the waitresses continued to argue back and forth, Jamie could tell this was getting nowhere. She asked them if any of the customers who'd been at the club last night were there now.

Sandy pointed out a couple of regulars standing at the bar. Jamie walked over to them and flashed her badge.

The two men recognized her and in unison said, "You're the chick who killed that psycho last night." Jamie nodded her head and asked them several questions. She basically got the same answers. Nobody really saw anything, and nobody knew the guy who had shot into the crowd.

Jamie's questions seemed to be getting her nowhere, so she decided to call the police lab and see if the autopsy on the gunman was finished. A lab technician named Stan answered the phone. Jamie asked him about the suspect—if the lab technicians had found anything unusual.

Stan told her that the guy was all hopped up on Rohypnol—"You know, the date-rape drug." He explained that the shooter had had enough of the drug in his system that he probably didn't know what he was doing at all.

Jamie hung up the phone and decided to go home. It had been a very long day. When she came to the stop sign on her street, another message scrawled in the same handwriting stared back at her. "Please stop him," it said.

She got out of her car and walked over to the sign. She reached up and touched it. She couldn't understand it. She felt a little crazy.

At home, she took a hot shower; the hot water felt good on her skin. She was very tired. She quickly dried her hair and went to bed.

When she woke in the morning, she thought the stop signs were all a dream. She felt like maybe this was a good thing. She went to the bathroom, brushed her hair and teeth, washed her face, and put on her makeup. After her morning routine of dressing and grabbing a Diet Coke from the refrigerator, she drove to work.

For the first time, she pulled into the detective side of the station's parking lot. As she walked through the station, she noticed a desk with her nameplate on it. For the first time, she felt really proud of herself for what she had accomplished. Jamie sat down at her desk and picked up the phone to make sure it worked. She opened all the drawers to see what was inside. She was like a kid in a candy store.

The police captain came by. "How is your investigation going?" he asked.

Jamie replied, "Not well. Nobody knows anything about this guy."

The captain handed her a file. "I want you to look this over. And I'm going to put you with a partner on this one. You can finish up that other case in your spare time, if you have any."

Another detective walked over. The captain said, "This is Detective Nelson. He is a veteran of ten years, and you can learn a lot from him."

Jamie's first impression of Detective Nelson was that her new partner was a very rough-looking and intimidating individual. A grizzled veteran, his hair was turning gray, and he was a little overweight. He chewed gum, a habit, Jamie would learn, that was constant, and so sometimes he would smack the gum when he talked. The captain patted Detective Nelson on the back. He told Jamie that Nelson would take the lead on the case; she would help him with the investigation.

Detective Nelson sat down next to Jamie and started briefing her on the case. A local politician had been murdered, and there was little to go on, other than rumors and speculation. One rumor suggested the politician had been taking payoffs for an upcoming housing project. Another held that he'd had a mistress. They would have to investigate and find out if there was any truth to these rumors.

Jamie's adrenaline was flowing. Now this was a case; this was why she wanted to be a detective. The other case was now on the back burner. It seemed to be going nowhere, and Jamie was now ready to move on. She felt the captain was telling her this by giving her this new case.

Jamie went straight home after work. She was so excited that she didn't even glance at the stop signs. She ran into her house and started reading the files. She wanted to be ready in the morning. She studied most of the night and fell asleep in her chair.

It was raining the next morning when her alarm rang in her bedroom. She woke with a stiff neck from sleeping in the chair. She got up and took a quick shower. She couldn't wait to get to work and start on this new case.

While driving to work, she came upon some road construction. A flagman with a stop-and-go sign was letting about ten cars go at a time. She was fifth in line when he turned the stop sign around. Written in the bottom corner, "Stop trying to forget about Sally."

The flagman turned the sign around again, and it said, "Go."

She pulled forward, jamming on her brakes once she was beside the man with the sign. She got out and flashed her badge, ordering the man to turn the sign around. He did so, and "Stop" was the only word on the sign.

Jamie just shook her head and left in disgust. She felt she must be hallucinating.

She arrived at work and waited for Detective Nelson. When he arrived moments later, Jamie was sipping on a Diet Coke. He walked up to her desk and handed her three names and three addresses. He told her to interview these people and report back to him. He told her to be thorough, ask good questions, and take good notes. He then introduced her to Officer Garrison, who would assist her with the interview.

Dan Garrison was twenty-five years old. He was five foot eleven, very thin, and very enthusiastic. He'd been a policeman for four years and had a background in computers. He was going to take his detective test next month.

"We don't normally put a rookie detective with an officer, but in this case, we will make an exception. We are very shorthanded, and I have other cases that I am trying to finish up. You will keep me informed of your progress." Detective Nelson walked away.

Officer Garrison extended his hand and said, "It's an honor to be working with you, Detective Bell."

"You can call me Jamie," she said.

"My first name is Dan," he replied. "I read about the bar shooting. That must have been tough."

Jamie replied, "I really don't like to talk about it. I never fired my weapon at someone before, not to mention fatally."

Dan just nodded his head and said, "Let's get to work and catch a killer!"

Jamie could see that Officer Garrison was just as excited as she was about this opportunity.

They drove to the address of the first name on the list. They were to talk to the councilman's wife. They knocked on the door, and she answered.

She took a deep sigh and said, "Can I help you?"

Jamie said, "I'm Detective Bell, and this is Officer Garrison. We would like to talk to you about your husband's death."

She invited them in.

After a dozen questions or so, Jamie felt in her gut that the widow knew nothing and was just as shocked as everyone else that her husband had been killed.

Then Officer Garrison asked, "Could we have access to your husband's computer?"

Jamie looked at Officer Garrison, thinking, *Now that was a good question. Why didn't I think of that?*

The councilwoman's wife led them to her husband's office and pointed to his computer. "Be my guest," she said and left the room.

Officer Garrison sat down at the desk and turned on the computer. He asked Jamie to shut the door.

Jamie said, "That was a good idea. Do you know what you're doing?"

He replied, "I'm a computer geek from way back. I'll just nose around in this computer. If he has any skeletons hidden in here, maybe I can find them."

Jamie was amazed by the way Officer Garrison zipped right through the computer.

Finally, he said, "Well, what do we have here? It seems our councilman has been on a kiddy porn site. Let's just see what he was looking at."

Suddenly, pictures of young naked girls and boys popped up all over the screen—very young children. The kids couldn't have been older than five, six, or seven. Jamie asked if the councilman had made contact with any of these sites or talked to any users online. Officer Garrison dug deeper, searching and searching.

Suddenly, the councilman's wife came back into the room. Jamie stood in front of the screen so she couldn't see what was on. "Did you find anything that can help you?" the wife asked.

"This could take some time to go through," Jamie answered. "But with your permission, we'd like to take the computer with us and have our experts look at it. Maybe we can find something that would help us find your husband's killer." Jamie put her arm around the wife and walked her to the door. "Just give us a few minutes to turn it off and unplug it and save everything. We will return it to you in two to three days," she assured the councilman's wife, adding, "If there is anything else you can think of, ma'am, don't hesitate to call me." Jamie handed her one of her new business cards and pointed out her cell number.

By the time Jamie turned around, Officer Garrison already had disconnected the laptop when Jamie got back to their car, and Jamie questioned Officer Garrison about his computer knowledge. "I have never seen anyone go through the computer as fast as you did," she commented.

He replied, "My father was a computer analyst. He fixed them and worked on them, and he taught me how. If you give me enough time, I can find out anything that you're hiding on your computer."

"All right," Jamie said. "Take this computer home with you and go through it. Let's not say anything to Detective Nelson yet. We'll see if anything is there. Maybe we'll get lucky. Let's go see the next person on the list."

When they got to the address, no one was home. So they went to see the next person on the list. Jamie knocked on the door. A young, pretty woman answered.

"Are you Miss Drake?"

The woman nodded her head yes.

"Can we come in? We would like to talk to you about Councilman Adams."

The woman seemed reluctant, but she let them in anyway.

Jamie started questioning her, asking the usual questions, such as, "How did you know the councilman?"

With every question, the young woman seemed agitated and very scared, like she was hiding something. This didn't surprise Jamie. After all, according to the report, the young woman was rumored to have been having an affair with the councilman.

Finally, Jamie got straight to the point and asked her directly about the affair and whether the rumors were true.

The interviewee looked Jamie straight in the eye and said, "No."

"You know I can take you downtown where the questions will get really tough," Jamie said, "if I feel like you're withholding information from me."

The woman sat back in her chair and glared at Jamie for a second or two. She lit a cigarette and said, "You can't protect me from what I know; if I told you what I know, I'd be dead tomorrow. Did I ever sleep with the councilman? I answered that question. Now, did I help the councilman get what he wanted? The answer to that question is yes. But you have to find out what he wanted for me to answer that question."

Officer Garrison said, "Did the councilman like young boys and girls?"

The woman was now fidgeting in her chair, taking deep breaths and puffing away on her cigarette. She answered, "Let's just say he loved children and leave it at that."

Jamie's radio blared, "Detective Bell, please call the station immediately. The captain needs to talk to you immediately."

Jamie replied, "Ten-four." She went out into the hallway and called Captain Jackson.

He answered, "Detective Bell, did you know that, when you take evidence or in this case, a computer out of someone's home, you have to log it in with your superior officer, which, in this case, is Detective Nelson? So bring it into the station. Drop what you're doing. Tell the person you're interviewing now that you will call him or her back or see him or her tomorrow."

Jamie replied, "But Captain Jackson, this woman is hiding something. I believe if we press her just a little bit more, she'll give us some useful information."

"Well, you should have thought of that earlier," the captain replied, "before you took that computer out of the councilman's home. We can't bend the rules for anyone. Bring the computer in and tell the person you're interviewing not to go anywhere—not to leave town—that we will finish the interview tomorrow." He then hung up the phone.

Jamie went back inside.

Jamie turned to the woman they were interviewing. "We have to go back to the station now. Don't leave town. We will come back by tomorrow and finish this interview."

Officer Garrison had a puzzled look on his face. They both left the room and went out into the hallway, walking down to their car. Officer Garrison asked Jamie, "What are we doing? That woman was ready to crack. We needed to keep questioning her."

Jamie stopped in the doorway and said, "The captain said we needed to log this computer in at the station house."

"You're kidding, right?" Garrison replied. "We just stop right in the middle of questioning a possible suspect, who knew something more than she was telling? We should have taken her downtown."

Jamie answered, "I'm just doing what I was told. I'm sure the captain knows procedure."

Officer Garrison just shook his head. "Do you want me to make a copy of the hard drive and put it on a flash drive so we will have it?"

"I don't think that will be necessary," she replied. "I'm sure the computer will be safe at the police station."

They got back into their car and drove away. Back at the police station, Jamie told Officer Garrison to log the computer in with either Detective Nelson or the captain. "I have to go to the restroom," she added. "I will meet you back at my desk in ten minutes."

Officer Garrison stopped at his desk, opened the drawer, pulled out a flash drive, and plugged it into the computer laptop unit. He quickly copied its contents onto the flash drive. Something seemed a little fishy to him; he felt like the evidence on this computer was vital, and it needed to be backed up. After a couple of minutes, the copy was complete, and he walked over to Detective Nelson's desk. He looked around but didn't see the detective, so he walked over to the captain's office.

The captain was sitting at his desk. He said, "Is that the councilman's laptop?"

Officer Garrison said, "Yes."

The captain asked, "Did you look at anything on the computer?"

Officer Garrison nodded and said that he'd found some kiddy porn on the unit. "We didn't really have a whole lot of time to search through it without your permission, Captain."

"I would like to search it myself," the captain said. "We have experts who will go through this computer back and forth. When they evaluate it, we will give you the information. This is very important. We can't screw this up; the mayor is breathing down my back on this. That's why I wanted the computer brought here; it can't be compromised in any way."

Officer Garrison was satisfied with the captain's explanation as to why he wanted the computer brought to the station immediately. He could see how important this case was. Officer Garrison left the captain's office and walked back to Jamie's desk, where he took a seat. He was spinning around in her chair, thinking to himself that he might be in trouble for copying those files. He took the flash drive out of his pocket and looked around on her desk for a place to hide it. He could see Jamie coming down the hallway. A pencil holder on her desk held several pens and pencils in the cup. He pulled out the pens and pencils and placed the flash drive in the bottom of the cup. He put a folded-up napkin over the flash drive and formed it to fit the bottom of the cup and then pushed all the pens and pencils back in the cup.

Jamie walked up and asked, "Did you do it? Did you get the computer to the Detective Nelson or the captain?"

Officer Garrison nodded and said, "I gave it to the captain."

She asked if the captain was mad. "He sounded mad on the phone."

Garrison responded, "No he wasn't mad. He just really seemed concerned about the handling of this case. He said there was a lot of pressure on him from the mayor."

"Should I go talk to him?" Jamie asked.

Officer Garrison responded, "I don't think so. He's been very busy. Let's go try and interview the other suspect before we call it a day."

As they started to leave, a middle-aged woman with a little girl stopped Jamie and asked if she knew where Captain Jackson's office was. While Jamie pointed down the hallway and explained which way to turn, Officer Garrison asked the little girl what her name was.

In the cutest little girl voice, she replied, "My name is Sarah Ann Lavone Young. But Mom called me ..."

Captain Jackson stepped into the hallway and shouted, "Sarah, come here, baby."

Forgetting whatever she'd been about to tell Jamie, the little girl ran down the hallway and jumped into the captain's arms. He picked her up and held her for a second before waving at the middle-aged woman and shouting, "I got her. She's fine. I will see you tomorrow."

As the woman started to leave, Jamie asked. "Is that the captain's daughter?"

The woman replied, "Yes. I'm the nanny. I have a doctor's appointment this afternoon, so I brought Sarah by for him to watch."

Officer Garrison butted in. "The little girl said her last name was Young."

"She's a little confused," the nanny answered. "Her name was just changed to Jackson. The adoption went through a few weeks ago. Her biological father died when she was a baby, and now ...—her voice trembled a bit—"of course you know about what happened to her mother. She was killed by a drunk driver. So much tragedy in one little girl's life. But she is blessed with a great stepfather. He is wonderful with her. I have to run. I'm going to be late."

The nanny left the room with Officer Garrison and Jamie right behind her. While driving to see another suspect, the pair happened upon a grassfire that had broken out along the highway. Firefighters had placed a few caution signs along the highway. The first one just read, "Caution." The next one said, "Don't forget about Sally."

Jamie slammed on the brakes and turned to Officer Garrison. "Did you read that sign?"

"No," he replied.

She slammed the car into reverse, driving backward to the sign and hitting the brakes again. This time the sign read, "Don't drive into smoke."

The driver of a car behind Jamie honked his or her horn.

Officer Garrison said, "It's just a sign warning about smoke. They always put them out when there's a grassfire along the highway."

Jamie put the car back into drive and continued on to the suspect's house.

Officer Garrison kept asking her what that was all about. She just said it was nothing. "I thought it said something else. That's all."

Officer Garrison pressed the issue, "What do you mean something else?"

She just told him repeatedly to forget it.

As they arrived at the suspect's house, Officer Garrison said, "I don't know how you expect me to forget that we were driving down the highway doing fifty-five, and you slammed on the brakes and backed up on the highway to look at a sign. We nearly got rear-ended, and I'm just supposed to forget about that!"

She told him to shut up.

As they'd arrived at the house, they walked up to the door, and Officer Garrison rang the doorbell.

A very young man, who looked to be right out of college, answered.

Jamie said, "Were you the aid to Councilman Adams?"

The young man answered, "Yes, I was. Would you like to come in?"

After they followed him in, Officer Garrison said, "This is a nice, secluded place."

The young man answered, "It's my parents' place. I'm living here while they're at their other home in Arizona. They are planning to move to Arizona permanently, and they're letting me stay here until they decide what to do with this house."

Jamie continued with the questions. "Your name is Mark Stevens?"

He answered, "Yes."

After several follow-up questions, she asked if he knew Miss Drake. He bit his lip before he answered. "Yes, I knew her."

Jamie followed that question with another. "What was your relationship with the councilman?"

He paused and then said they were friends.

Officer Garrison spoke up and asked, "Was Miss Drake sleeping with him?"

Mark shook his head no. "She helped him with certain things."

"Certain things," Garrison replied. "Explain yourself."

The young man started biting his lip again, fidgeting in his seat as if he wanted to say something, but he knew he couldn't. "I don't know," he finally said. "He would call her when he needed something. That's what he told me—that she had certain talents and that she could get him anything," Jamie said.

"I feel like you're lying to me," she said as she leaned in. She raised her eyebrows and folded her arms. "You know we can take you downtown. We can hold you in a cell for forty-eight hours for questioning. You had to have seen something. We can protect you. Tell us what you know."

The young man just sat there, not saying a thing.

Jamie stood up and said, "Cuff this little prick. We're taking him downtown. He can sweat it out in a cell!"

The young man spoke up and started rambling on and on, saying that he had seen things. "Things that weren't quite right," he started. "Children, young children; pictures, naked pictures. He shouldn't have had those, but he did. And it was something to do with Miss Drake. I knocked over a file. It had pictures of boys and girls in it. It was an accident. The next day, he was dead. I don't know what happened. She was there that day. She brought him the pictures. I know it. I know it," he repeated, tears rolling down his face.

Jamie looked at Officer Garrison and said, "I think we got what we wanted here." She then turned to the young man and said, "Don't leave town. Do you feel safe here?"

He answered, "Yes. No one knows I'm here, at least no one at the office does. I told the police they could reach me here."

Officer Garrison said, "Stay put and keep a low profile."

It was nearly dark when Jamie and Officer Garrison got back into the car. Jamie considered going to Drake's apartment, but as it grew later and later, and they waited in backed up traffic, she decided to hold off until morning. "I'll drop you off at the station," she told her partner. "We'll hit it again first thing in the morning."

Officer Garrison agreed; it was getting late, and he didn't want his wife to worry. When they arrived at the station, it had started to rain. Officer Garrison got out of the car and told Jamie he would see her in the morning. Jamie parked and went inside. She decided to get started on a report of what had happened during the day while everything was fresh in her mind. She was working at her desk when she heard footsteps behind her.

She turned suddenly, and there was Sarah. "Hi, what are you doing?" the little girl asked.

She is so cute, Jamie thought. Sarah had blonde hair and green eyes and little, cute dimples when she smiled. She couldn't have been more than five or six years old. "I'm doing my reports," Jamie told her. "What are you doing?"

"I'm here with my daddy. We're going to eat."

"That's right," said Captain Jackson as he approached the pair. "We're going to eat. Would you like to come?"

Jamie stuttered when she spoke. "I have all this paperwork."

"That paperwork can wait till morning," he said. "Come have a bite to eat with us. I insist. It would be nice to have a conversation with an adult."

"Fine," she replied. "Where are we going?"

The little girl shouted, "McDonald's. McDonald's!"

"Well, McDonald's it is," Jamie answered.

The police captain just rolled his eyes and said, "Fine."

The trio piled into the captain's car. He carefully put Sarah in her safety seat, and Sarah sang a song she had learned in school.

They walked into the restaurant, ordered their food, and sat down. Within a few minutes, a pretty young Latino woman brought their food to them. Sarah immediately tore into her Happy Meal. The police captain asked Jamie about what had happened today. Jamie informed him all that had happened and how she thought that the suspect, Miss Drake, was the key. She told him she planned to go by her apartment in the morning and either bring her in for questioning or just question her more there. "What do you think would be better?" she asked.

"Maybe you should bring her into the station," he suggested. "That way we can hold her and protect her."

The conversation drifted away from work. As Jamie looked at the police captain, she thought to herself, *This is a handsome man, and he seems so at ease with the young child.* Jamie was flattered that a police captain would take an interest in her career. She felt very comfortable with him, so she decided to open up a little. She told him about the stop signs, that she felt like someone was trying to get a message to her that a little girl named Sally was in trouble. "It must be a product of my imagination," she concluded.

He listened very carefully to everything she had to say, and after she was through, he said, "You never know. Sometimes strange things happen for a reason. I would just keep my eyes and ears open, and if you get any new information on this young girl, come to me. Maybe we can investigate. But at this time, I know for a fact there are no missing children named Sally or no complaints from a parent or guardian with a child named Sally."

The meal was now over. Sarah grabbed Jamie by the hand and said, "Come play with me in the balls. Please, please."

Jamie looked over at her captain, who said, "Do whatever you want."

She just smiled at the captain and ran with Sarah and jumped into a big pile of balls. After about fifteen minutes or so, Jamie was exhausted. She told the little girl she needed to go home and get some rest. As she helped Sarah out of the balls, she noticed what looked like a burn on the girl's back. It was very small. She asked Sarah about it. Sarah didn't know anything about it.

The police captain walked over to the screen that partitioned the playroom from the rest of the restaurant and hollered for Sarah and Jamie to come out. It was getting pretty close to Sarah's bedtime.

Jamie gave Sarah a hug. Then they drove back to the police station in captain's car, where Sarah soon fell asleep.

Jamie started to get out of the car, but her captain stopped her. "This was nice," he said. "Maybe in six months to a year we can do this again, if you want to. I won't be ready to see anyone for at least that amount of time. Maybe we can just be friends with no expectations at all because I feel like I'm going to be very lonely for a while. I miss my wife, and if I just need to talk to someone who's an adult, maybe you won't mind."

Jamie looked at him and smiled. "Any time, Captain," she said, "anytime."

"My name is Richard when we're off duty," he replied. But on duty I'm still Captain Jackson." He winked at her.

She smiled back and waved as he drove away.

She started to go inside and finish up her work, but, realizing that she was very tired, she got in her car and drove home. Nonchalantly, she glanced at the familiar stop sign near her home. Once again it said, "Stop Raping Sally." She again tried to put the sign out of her mind.

At home, she took a shower, went to bed, and turned the radio on, hoping it would clear her mind. She was able to fall asleep, but every night she had the same recurring dream about a small girl in trouble. It haunted her every night's sleep lately.

CHAPTER 3

She woke in the morning having had very little sleep. She wanted to get to work early to finish the paperwork she had started last night. While driving to work, Jamie got a phone call on her cell. It was Officer Garrison; he yelled frantically in the phone, "She's gone. I went by her apartment this morning on the way to work. She wasn't there. Her apartment was pretty messed up."

Jamie asked, "How did you get in?"

He answered, "The door was open. I just walked right in. I believe she was taken against her will—maybe even murdered. We need to get ballistics to the crime scene. Maybe there are some clues that were left behind."

"Let's tell Detective Nelson what happened so he can report to the captain before we go any further—stay there!" she shouted. "I'll meet you there!" Jamie immediately told Detective Nelson what happened, who told her pick up Officer Garrison and get Mark Stevens."

"He may be in trouble; bring him in and we will put him in protective custody!" Detective Nelson said.

Jamie put on the siren for the first time in a while. She picked up Officer Garrison and then drove like a madwoman to Mark Stevens's house.

When they arrived, they found that the door had been kicked in. They pulled their weapons and proceeded in cautiously. Jamie hollered, "Police! Mark, are you here?"

They walked around the room looking for Mark. There he lay on the floor. His computer was still on. His soccer balls screensaver was bouncing back and forth. Jamie reached and felt his neck for a pulse. She didn't find one. Officer Garrison moved the mouse on Mark's computer screen, and a kiddy porn site popped up on the screen. A bottle of pills lay under Mark. Someone wanted this to look like a suicide. This was Jamie's first thought.

"I don't buy it," Jamie said. Opening up some of the drawers in the desk, she found magazines with pictures of young boys and girls.

"I don't believe this," Officer Garrison said. "This is just too perfect."

"We'd better call this in," Jamie said. She knelt down and looked at Mark Stevens's face. "His face is bruised," she noted. "It looks like he's been hit several times. I think somebody's covering something up or tying up loose ends, Officer."

Jamie then called Detective Nelson on his cell phone. She told him what they had found. Detective Nelson told them to stay there, and he would send a team over there to check out the house. While driving back to the station it started to rain again, and when it rained traffic was slow, which gave Jamie and Officer Garrison more time to talk about the case. Officer Garrison started rambling on and on, saying he thought this was a massive cover-up—that somebody wanted all these people dead. And he thought maybe there would be something on the councilman's computer to prove his theory.

Jamie answered, "I think it's a little simpler than that. I think it's a kiddy porn ring."

After they'd both rambled on and on, trying to prove their theories to one another, they finally arrived at the police station. Detective Nelson met them as they walked through the door. He said, "The captain wants to see all of us—now!"

The three walked into the captain's office, Detective Nelson shutting the door behind him. You could see it in his face; the captain was angry. He looked them over one at a time before speaking. He shouted at all of them as spit flew from his mouth, "I'm losing confidence in all of you. The mayor is breathing down my neck on this case. He wants it solved and somebody in jail, and all we're turning up is more dead bodies."

Officer Garrison spoke. "We don't know that Miss Drake is dead, Captain."

Pointing his finger at Officer Garrison, the captain told him to shut up. Garrison was the low man on the totem pole on this case. "I don't want you to speak," the captain said. "Miss Drake is missing, right? Her apartment was a mess, and we found traces of blood. So shut your pie hole!"

He then turned to Jamie, "Maybe I shouldn't have put a rookie detective on this case. You're going to have to do a better job to keep that detective badge of yours, Detective Bell."

He asked Jamie and Officer Garrison to leave his office. As they shut the door behind them, they heard him screaming at Detective Nelson. "You're the senior detective on this case. It has been run sloppily. This all falls on your head. You better clean it up and take more of a lead on this case, or I will put somebody else on it!"

Detective Nelson left his office, motioning for Jamie and Officer Garrison to follow him. He went to the evidence room and pointed at a large file cabinet. "See that cabinet right there?" he said. "Those are the councilman's files. I want you to go through every piece of paper in that cabinet, and if you find something, I want you to hand it to me. And I will tell you if you have found something. And after you are finished here, I will find something else for you to do on this case." He slammed the door behind him.

Jamie looked at Officer Garrison. "This could take a week," she said. "I guess we're being punished."

Garrison agreed, and they went to work on the files. The work was very slow paced, and the day seemed to drag on forever. At five o'clock, it was time to go home.

Officer Garrison said, "I'm going to go. I guess I'll see you in the morning in here."

"Okay, see you in the morning." Jamie continued looking through the cabinet, hoping to find something that would restore Detective Nelson's confidence in her.

About an hour later, the door opened. Captain Jackson said, "You still here? Would you like to have dinner with me and my daughter again?"

Jamie gave the captain a "go to hell" look and said, "You bawl me out for doing a bad job and then you expect me to just forget everything and go to dinner with you and your daughter!"

The captain smiled and said, "Look, I have to kick ass around here to get things done. If you can't take it, maybe you shouldn't be a detective. You have to do your work from nine to five and, after that, forget about it, or this job will eat you alive. Detective Nelson is one of my best friends. He knows I'm just doing my job, and you have to realize that too. So I'll ask again, do you want to have dinner with my daughter and me? This is not a date. I'm not hitting on you because you're an attractive woman. You have to eat, so eat with us."

Sarah poked her head around the door and said, "McDonald's, McDonald's. I want McDonald's."

Jamie looked at those big, green eyes and said, "Is that the only place you like to eat?"

The little girl nodded her head and said, "Uh huh. I love McDonald's."

Jamie said, "Okay, let's go."

On the drive over to McDonald's, the little girl told Jamie that her name was like a song they sung at school at Christmastime. She started laughing and singing the song, "Jamie Bell, Jamie Bell, Jamie all the way." It was so cute. Jamie and Richard couldn't stop laughing, and Sarah continued with the song "Jingle Bells" all the way to McDonald's.

By the time they sat down to eat, Jamie had gotten over the criticism that Captain Jackson had given her earlier in the day.

"You seem in a better mood," Richard noted, "but my daughter brings that out in everyone."

"She's so cute," Jamie whispered. "But with all the tragedy in her life, how do you keep her so happy, Captain?"

He interrupted her and said, "It's after work. My name is Richard, not Captain."

She apologized and said, "Okay, Richard."

"She has always been a happy little girl, ever since I've known her. I'm interested in where you think this case is leading us."

She thought for a minute and then said, "I have a feeling it has something to do with a kiddy porn ring of some kind. It could be small; it could be big. But that's my feeling on the case. Officer Garrison thinks it's bigger than that. He thinks it's politically motivated, that someone high up is eliminating these people that could lead back to him or her."

"He is way out there," Richard responded. "I hope you don't feel like I yelled at him too much, but he is young and brash. He has to learn when to speak his mind. What do you think of him?"

"I think he's very intelligent, and he's quite the computer whiz. There is not much he can't do on a computer. I think it would be to your advantage to let him analyze the computer information on the councilman's computer. He was only on the councilman's computer for a minute and had already pulled up information that was leading to the kiddy porn sites. I was amazed," she said.

Richard sat back in his chair and took a drink of his soda. "He might be good, but we have some excellent people looking into it."

Sarah then came over to Jamie, grabbed her hand, and said, "Hey, Jingle Bells, let's go play in the balls. Come on."

"Okay, let's go," Jamie replied.

As little Sarah pulled Jamie by the hand toward the jumping balls, Richard watched them walk away. He leaned forward, staring at Jamie's ass. *Very nice*, he thought.

After Jamie and Sarah had played for about fifteen minutes, Richard walked up to the ball cage. He said, "Sarah, we need to go. You and Jamie need to come out now."

As Jamie lifted little Sarah out of the balls, she noticed a slight burn on Sarah's back again. She helped Sarah put her shoes on and walked over to Richard. "I noticed a slight burn on her back," she said. "You know how she got that?"

"It was my fault," he answered. "I felt so stupid. I was smoking a cigar, and I was carrying her over my shoulder to bed. We were playing. It's one of those stupid things. She kind of rolled into the cigar as I was walking up the stairs, and the cigar burned her on the back. I felt terrible. It was one of the first nights we were alone, after her mother had died. At that moment, I felt I was an awful parent. The adoption had just gone through, and I burned my daughter. Thank you for noticing. It proves you're a good detective. You have to notice the little things sometimes to figure out a case."

The threesome drove back to the station, and Richard and Sarah dropped Jamie off. Little Sarah yelled out, "Good-bye, Jingle Bells." She laughed as they drove away. Jamie could hear her singing "Jingle Bells" again.

Inside the police station, Jamie headed back to the file room. She hadn't been sleeping much anyway, so she figured she might as well do a little more work and try and get ahead on this case. Maybe she'd find something. She stopped at the vending machine, dropped some change into the slot, and got a diet soda. Then she sat down at the filing cabinet and started poring through the files.

After about an hour or so, she fell asleep. She dreamed again of a small girl crying out for her mommy. It was raining and very windy. She could hear lightning and thunder. She awoke to a gunshot in the dream.

It was now four fifteen in the morning, and she had to be at work at seven. There wasn't much sense in her going home. She went to the bathroom, washed her face, and then went back to the vending machine and got herself another diet soda. She headed back to the file room. There had to be something, anything, and so she kept looking.

At about ten minutes till seven, Officer Garrison walked in. He said, "You look like shit. You have been here all night!"

"Most of the night," she answered. "I fell asleep in my chair for several hours."

He said, "You can't score any Brownie points by staying here all night unless you found something."

She just shook her head, "No, I haven't found anything."

"This is a waste of time," he answered. "We should be studying the councilman's computer. I'm telling you; there's evidence there!"

"Well, we don't have the computer, so there's nothing we can do," she shot back.

"Well, maybe we do, and maybe we don't," he replied.

"What do you mean by that?" she asked.

He kind of smiled and said, "I made a copy. It's in a safe place. I copied it on a flash drive and hid it, just in case, because I bet the lab doesn't find nothing on that computer or somehow it gets damaged and they lose all the files."

Just then, Detective Nelson walked up to them. "We have gotten the readout on that computer of the councilman's. There wasn't a lot, but there was some evidence there. We think it is some kiddie porn ring of some kind. We came up with a phone number. You have to call and leave a message, and someone will get back to you—they call on a different pay phone every time, so it can be very hard to trace. Against my better judgment, you two are going undercover. We are going to provide you with pictures of young children. You two are going to try and make a sale of a young child on this number.

"Don't worry. We have an undercover officer who can pose as a child. He's a little person, a midget. We are going to borrow him from another station. When it comes to making the sale or the drop, we are going to provide you with an apartment. You'll make a call from there. You can't screw this up."

He handed Jamie two pieces of paper. "This is your script, the story you will tell to this scumbag. Stay with this script and don't make any changes. You need to be at the address on this piece of paper in about two hours, and an officer will be there to wire you and show you how to activate the wire. You need to go down to the motor pool and pick up an unmarked car. Be sure to get an older car because you are a scumbag. Remember that; act like it." Detective Nelson turned and walked away.

Officer Garrison gave Jamie a high five and yelled out, "Undercover work. Yeah, baby! Yeah, baby! That's what I'm talking about!" He was so excited he said, "I have to go pee. I'll meet you downstairs in the motor pool."

Downstairs, Jamie and Officer Garrison were given a car. They drove to the apartment and walked upstairs. They used the key Officer Nelson had given them to open the apartment. Another officer was already there hooking up the phone line. He explained how it worked and how they were supposed to use it. He pointed to the closet where some old clothes were. "Now try and keep a low profile," he said. "Call the number in about an hour and wait until they call you back."

About an hour later, Officer Garrison made the call. An answering machine picked up. He left a message and number.

Jamie and Garrison sat in the cramped apartment all day and didn't get one phone call. At about five o'clock, Officer Garrison called into the station and asked for Detective Nelson. "No call yet," he told the detective.

"You will just have to stay there a day or two until someone calls. And if no one calls, we might have to try something else. These things take time. You've got to be patient. Check back in the morning." Detective Nelson hung up the phone.

Officer Garrison put his cell phone back in his pocket and looked at Jamie. He said, "This sucks. We don't even have a TV."

Jamie said, "Why don't you go get us something to eat. I'll wait by the phone. Remember, you are a scumbag, so act like one." She laughed.

Officer Garrison went downstairs. Jamie was glad because he was driving her crazy. All he did was pace the floor and check the phone.

CHAPTER 4

About thirty minutes later he came back with the food and a radio. She asked, "Where did you get that?"

"I bought it from a guy who was selling them on the street. We have to have something to listen to."

When they finished eating, he turned on the radio and asked what she wanted to listen to.

Jamie replied, "It doesn't matter—anything but rap."

Garrison found a station. Then the phone rang. He tripped over the cord of the radio and pulled it out of the wall as he raced to the phone. He answered in a low voice, trying to sound like he was stoned.

The person on the other end of the line said, "Did you leave a message?"

Officer Garrison said, "Yes."

The caller said, "I will call you back later," and hung up the phone.

Garrison turned to Jamie and said, "What the hell was that?"

He hung up the phone then knelt down and picked up his radio, which was now broken. He said, "I paid twenty-five dollars for this radio. Shit! My wife is going to kill me for spending my allowance on a radio that I broke minutes after I bought it."

Jamie said, "Are you afraid of your wife?"

He answered, "No, she just handles all the money. She gives me an allowance every week. She's an accountant. She's good with numbers."

Jamie just said, "Maybe. Why don't you get some sleep? I'll sit by the phone and wake you up in a few hours."

He agreed, and Jamie laid her head on the desk by the phone. Officer Garrison went back into the bedroom and lay down on the mattress.

It was two o'clock in the morning when the phone rang. Jamie had fallen asleep with her head on the table. She jumped up and ran into the next room to wake up Officer Garrison. She grabbed his shoulder and shook it and told him to get up, that the phone was ringing. He stumbled to the phone and answered.

The voice on the other end said, "I hear you have something to sell."

Garrison answered, "Yes I do."

"Do you have pictures?" the voice asked.

"Yes," Garrison replied.

"Bring the pictures to the phone booth at Twenty-Third and Maple, lay them under the phone book, and I will see if there are any takers. Do you have a number in mind?"

Officer Garrison stuttered and said, "No, I don't know, whatever the going rate is. I need money, and I need it quickly."

The voice said, "Don't we all," then hung up.

Officer Garrison told Jamie, "We have to make a drop now." He told her where.

"I'll leave now and meet you there," she said. "I'll find a place where I can watch the phone from a distance."

Officer Garrison nodded his head and said, "Go. I'll leave in fifteen minutes."

Jamie went out the back door. She checked her gun to make sure it was loaded, knowing she'd be walking alone in a bad part of town. The phone booth was two blocks away, but she didn't go directly there. She took a long route, thinking somebody would be watching the phone booth. She found an all-night donut shop with a view of the phone booth. She stopped to order a donut and a diet soda and sat down watching the phone.

Within five minutes, Officer Garrison walked up and stepped into the phone booth. He pulled out the envelope from his jacket and carefully placed it underneath the phone book, shut the door, and walked down the street toward the apartment.

As Jamie ate her donut, she waited patiently. A group of young men walked up to the donut shop. There must have been six or seven of them. They stood in front of the door so Jamie could not see the phone booth. She stood up so she could see, but her view was still obstructed, so she walked outside. The phone booth door was now open.

One of the young men hooted, "Hey, baby, are you looking for a date?"

Jamie responded, "Shut up, punk!"

He grabbed her by the arm and pulled her close to him. He said, "Now, you really want me to give it to you, don't you baby?"

As soon as the kid had grabbed her, Jamie had reached for her weapon. Now she stuck it in his crotch. She whispered in his ear, "You better let me go quickly, or I'll blow your dick right off, baby!"

The young man could feel the pistol against his body. He whispered back, "Take it easy. I was just playin'."

"I'm not!" she whispered back.

He let her go, and she ran toward the phone booth. The pictures were gone. She pretended to be looking through the phone book and made a call. She called her own house, thinking that if somebody was watching her, she better act like she was on the phone. After a couple minutes of pretending to talk to somebody on her answering machine, she hung up the phone and walked the long way back to the apartment.

When she arrived, Officer Garrison wasn't there. She was now officially worried. What if something had happened to him? Then she heard someone walking up the stairs.

Officer Garrison walked through the door with a cup of coffee and a magazine in his hand. "Did you see anyone?" he asked.

"My view got blocked," she explained. "Someone got in the phone booth and got the pictures. They must've been watching you. I guess we just wait and see if they call. I'm going to lie down. You wait by the phone this time."

Feeling very tired, Jamie lay down. She put her gun under the pillow.

She had just started to doze off when Jamie heard the door knob jiggle and then what sounded like a gun clip being slapped in. Suddenly the apartment door was kicked in. A man jumped into the doorway and sprayed the apartment with machine-gun fire.

CHAPTER 5

Jamie rolled off the bed and crawled under it. She didn't know if Officer Garrison had been hit. She could hear footsteps and could smell the lead from the gunfire. The shooter kicked the bedroom door open and sprayed the room. All she could see was black Nike tennis shoes and baggy jeans. She fired four times into his legs and feet. He fell to the floor screaming in pain and agony, and for a moment, he could see her under the bed. Before he could shoot again, she shot him twice in the head.

She crawled out from under the bed. Officer Garrison lay behind the couch. He'd been hit two to three times but was still alive. She radioed for an ambulance. "Officer down," she announced. "Officer down."

At that moment, the phone rang. Jamie answered. The voice on the phone said, "This isn't my first rodeo. I know when a couple of cops are trying to hustle me. Don't bother trying to trace the guy you killed back to me. I used him, just like you used your partner, and he's probably dead." The caller was laughing as he hung up the phone.

Jamie slammed the phone down. She could hear the emergency vehicles getting closer. She tried to stop the bleeding by grabbing some napkins and placing them on her partner's wounds. He had been hit in the leg, butt, and shoulder. His breathing was steady, but he was unconscious. He must have hit his head on the floor or something, Jamie determined. He had a big knot on his head.

The other police officers arrived, and the EMTs dressed Garrison's wounds. While the officer was still unconscious, the paramedic gave Jamie the thumbs up, assuring her that Officer Garrison would be fine.

Jamie reached inside a pocket of Officer Garrison's, pulled out his cell phone, and dialed the last number called. His wife answered. Jamie told her what had happened and that her husband was fine. He was unconscious, but he was fine. She told her what hospital he would be taken to, saying that she would meet her there.

Officer Garrison's wife was waiting for Jamie when the ambulance brought him in. She ran to the gurney's side, moving with it down the hallway and grabbing her husband's hand. Finally, a nurse stopped her and told her she would have to wait there while the doctor worked on her husband. She just stood there, staring at the door.

Jamie laid a comforting hand on her partner's wife's shoulder and steered her gently to the waiting room. She told his wife what had happened and said again that Officer Garrison was going to be fine. "He was lucky," she said.

Captain Richard Jackson walked in. He pulled Jamie to the side and asked her what had happened. She described the scene to him in full detail.

"Imagine that," he said, "you ending up under a bed and killing someone—just like at the bar when you were under the pool table. Do you know anything about the guy you killed?"

She said she didn't. Detective Nelson was checking him out now. She told him about the phone call she'd gotten right after the shooting.

"So you think this guy was just a patsy?"

"Yes I do," Jamie said.

"What's our next move, Detective?"

"I haven't really thought about that yet, Captain," she answered. "I'm just worried about Garrison."

He nodded and said, "Yes. That's where our thoughts should be right now. You stay here until you get some word on Officer Garrison. I will speak with Detective Nelson to plan our next move. Call me in the morning, or just come in, or better yet, take a few days off. Check in with the psychiatrist; make sure you are in the right frame of mind before you come back to work!

"No," she said, "I'd rather work the case and stay busy."

He just nodded and walked over to Mrs. Garrison. He said a few kind words and held her hand before leaving the hospital.

Two hours later, a doctor came out and called for Mrs. Garrison. She ran to him, her eyes bloodshot and her nose runny. She'd been crying ever since Officer Garrison had disappeared into the operating room, worrying about her husband.

The young doctor took her by the hand and told her that her husband would be fine. "None of the wounds were life-threatening. He should be able to go home in two or three days. You can see him now. He should be waking up any time now."

She thanked him and asked which room her husband was in. She picked up her jacket and went immediately to the room.

Jamie thanked the doctor too and followed her. When Jamie pushed open the door, Garrison's wife was already sitting on his bed, holding his hand and rubbing his face, and asking him to please wake up. "Open your eyes and talk to me," she implored.

In a few minutes, he did. His first words were, "Am I okay?"

His wife said, "Yes. You're going to be fine."

He whispered, "What about Jamie, Detective Bell?"

His wife pointed and said, "She's right over there."

Jamie walked up to his bedside and said, "Hey, partner, you sure know how to take a bullet. That crazy guy didn't hit one main artery on you."

While laughing, he asked, "Did you get him?"

"Yes," she answered. "I got him!"

Jamie went back to the waiting room. She decided she would stay there tonight, since she wasn't sleeping much anyway. She was a little upset. She had killed again, and for what reason? This was the part of the job she hated the most, trying to make sense of killing a human being. But most of it was instinct, self-preservation. She hoped it would never happen again, but she knew—or at least she felt—that if she ever had to face down the owner of that voice on the phone, it would happen again.

The next morning, she woke in the chair in the waiting room. She checked on Officer Garrison. The doctor told her again that her partner was fine, so she went to work. It was still early in the morning. She went to her desk, got a toothbrush out of one of her drawers, and went to the ladies' room. She brushed her teeth, washed her face, and put her hair up in a ponytail.

When the steam rose from the hot water, fogging the mirror, the words "Stop Raping Sally" appeared. She immediately took a few steps backward and glared at the mirror. After frantically wiping the mirror off with a paper towel, she went to the bathroom stall, sat down on the toilet, pulled her feet up, and cried. She didn't really know what she was crying about. Was she crying about the little girl who was in trouble? Or was she the little girl who was in trouble? Was she in over her head on this case?

A knock on the bathroom stall door startled her. Then she heard Captain Jackson's voice. "Jamie, is that you?" he asked. "Are you all right?"

She cleared her throat and said, "Yes."

"It's perfectly natural to be upset after killing someone and your partner being shot," he said gently. "Open the door."

She got up and opened the door.

He stepped inside, closed the door behind him, and locked it. He pulled her close and hugged her. At first she resisted, but her emotions got the better of her, and she just let go and cried uncontrollably in his arms. He kept saying, "It's okay. You did nothing wrong." After a minute or so, he let her go. "You will be fine," he said. "You're stronger than you think; sometimes you just need a good cry. I know I did when my wife was shot. I cried for hours. Why don't you go home?"

"I'm better off here working than sitting home alone," she insisted.

"Okay stay here. We'll find something for you to do. I'll talk to Detective Nelson when he gets in. Any luck with that file cabinet of the councilman's?"

She just shook her head no. "We've found nothing so far."

"You can always go back in there. That'll keep you busy."

She nodded and said okay, and he left the bathroom. She washed her face again and went to the file room to start combing through the councilman's files again.

At lunchtime, Jamie decided to go to the hospital and see her partner. When she arrived, he was sitting up in his bed eating his lunch. "Look who's here," he said. "It's about time you came to see me." Officer Garrison then took a sip of water and said, "I wanted to thank you for taking care of that guy. Any news on him—who he was or anything?"

She shook her head no. "All we know so far is he's a small-time thief who had opened fire on us. We can't connect him with anybody."

"It makes no sense," Garrison replied. "Well, at least you killed the bastard before he killed me. And I want to thank you for that." He then pushed the button to raise the bed a little higher, and Jamie shoved another pillow behind his back so he could sit up better. "So did they put you behind the desk or you just been hanging out at home?"

"I've been looking through the councilman files, trying to stay busy."

Jamie's cell phone started ringing. It was Captain Jackson. "Hello," she answered.

"Where are you?" he asked.

After she told him where she was, he said, "I have very interesting news for you. Maybe you should come to my office. I have something I want to show you."

Jamie said she'd be there in fifteen minutes. She hung up her phone and told Officer Garrison she would see him later.

"What was the call about?" he asked.

She told him she didn't know yet.

When she arrived in the captain's office, he told her to shut the door. "This came over the wire today," he said. "I think this will have special interest for you. A little girl is missing. Social services just now reported it to us. She is six years old, her first name is Amber, and her last name is Sally."

Jamie's eyes got as big as saucers.

The captain said, "I thought you would be interested in this. Maybe this is what your nightmares are about. And you're not going to believe this. This girl has no family. We interviewed the girlfriend of the thief who shot at you, and she told Detective Nelson that the guy had kidnapped a girl and sold her to someone for five thousand dollars. The girlfriend had half of the money, and he told her he would get the other half after he did another little job last night. She didn't know what the job was, but we figure it was killing you and Officer Garrison last night at the apartment.

"Maybe this little girl's mother is sending you messages or dreams to help her little girl. I know it sounds far-fetched, but stranger things have happened, and I've seen stranger things. I want you to go down to social services and find out anything you can on this little girl. I have a bad feeling that this guy who called you has her, and God only knows what he's doing to her."

Captain Jackson told Jaime she would be better talking to social services than he would since she was a woman. "You're more sensitive to these things than men are."

Jamie now had a clearer focus on this case. She went downstairs and drove directly to the social services office. She asked for the person in charge of the missing child and was told to go to room 224 and talk to a Mrs. Jordan.

When Jamie arrived at the door, she knocked, and Mrs. Jordan said, "Come on in."

Jamie walked into the room, and a woman in her sixties asked Jamie to sit down.

Jamie started questioning the woman about the missing girl. The woman told Jamie how tragic Amber Sally's disappearance was. "It seems she has fallen through the cracks of the system. She has no family at all. She was in her bed at lights out at our children's facility or orphanage." She then wrinkled her nose and said, "We really don't like that word—orphanage—anymore. Then she was gone in the morning. We can't explain it. We first thought she had run away, but when we found that two of our security cameras were damaged, we called the police. There was no forcible entry in our facility. It was like she just vanished."

Jamie then asked to see all the video from the security cameras for the last three days, including the outside video. Mrs. Jordan was way ahead of Jamie. She already had all the tapes on her desk. She pointed to them and said, "We have already looked at them with our security officers. But we would gladly turn them over to you, hoping you could find something." She grabbed a small bag, put the tapes and a computer disk in it, and handed them to Jamie. "You might need these too—employment records and photos of everyone who has worked here in the last six months."

As Jamie started to leave, Mrs. Jordan said, "I hope you can find something. She was a sweet little girl, and I fear the worst." A couple of tears rolled down the woman's face. Jamie could see Mrs. Jordan was very sincere and very worried.

This time, Jamie went straight home. She was not going to log the tapes in just yet, as she wanted to get a look at them first. She decided to stop by the hospital and give the computer disk to Officer Garrison.

"We have a new lead." She explained to him about the little girl who was missing. Handing him the disk, she said, "I figured since you are a computer nerd, you could look through this while you're in the hospital. Do you have your laptop here?"

He said he did.

"I'm going home to review these videotapes to see if I can find anything before I turn them over to the captain," she told him.

"Good idea!" he agreed.

At home, she went straight to her TV and put the first tape in her VCR. She watched the tape very carefully, but she didn't see anything out of the ordinary. She put the second tape in and was watching it when she noticed the clock on the bottom of the tape. There was a gap—a five-minute gap. The clock stopped at 1:16 a.m. and started up again at 1:21 a.m. Someone had to have turned the tape off for five minutes. On the video showing the outside of the facility at the same time, a dark-colored van in the parking lot. You couldn't read a license plate, but it definitely looked out of place. She found another time lapse from 12:33 a.m. until 1:27 a.m. "That's almost an hour," she said to herself. The security guard—it had to be the security guard. He would be the only one who could turn the cameras off at the main terminal.

She picked up her cell phone and called Officer Garrison. She asked him to search the files she'd left and find out which security guard was on duty the night the little girl vanished.

Within a moment, he had the answer. "It says here Roberts—James Roberts. And he is on duty right now. They do a rotating shift."

She asked if he had found anything else on the files.

He had. "I want you to guess who used to work at the orphanage."

"Who?" she asked.

"Sherrie Drake. There's a picture in the file, and it's the same Sherrie Drake we interviewed the other day."

"Great job!" Jamie said. "I'm calling Detective Nelson right now to see if he will meet me over at the social service center to interview this security guard."

She hung up and immediately called Detective Nelson. She told him what she had found out and asked him to meet her at the facility. He told her he would, and a few minutes later, they went to the security office.

A guard was sitting in the security office, viewing the cameras. Detective Nelson walked in, flashed his badge, and asked the guard if his name was James Roberts.

"Yes," he said. "What's this about?"

"It's about the little girl who went missing the other night," Detective Nelson replied. "She disappeared on your shift, right?"

"Yes," he replied. "I already told the police everything I know!"

Detective Nelson picked him up by the shirt collar and slammed him against the wall. He said, "Look, dick weed, you either tell me why there is almost an hour of missing tape and why the camera was turned off, or I'm taking you downtown and charging you with kidnapping!"

Now frightened, the security guard started spilling his guts. "I turned the camera off," he said.

"Why?" Jamie yelled.

"This girl I used to date came by to see me, and I let her in."

Detective Nelson asked, "What's her name?"

"Sherrie," Roberts replied. "Sherrie Drake."

Detective Nelson let the security guard go, sticking his finger in the scared man's face. "You better not be lying to me," he snarled. "Did you know Sherrie's in trouble and the police are looking for her?"

"No!" Roberts insisted.

"Well, what did she want?" Detective Nelson asked.

He answered, "She told me she missed me, and we had a couple of drinks. Then something happened."

"What happened?" Detective Nelson asked.

"Well, one thing led to another," Roberts started, "and the next thing I know, we're having sex right here on my desk—I mean wild, animal sex. She did things to me I'd never had done to me before. "Look, I'm no Tom Cruise," he added. "When a good-looking woman like that comes on to me, I'm going to jump all over it!"

"How can you prove this?" Jamie demanded.

"I made a copy of the tape," he replied. "It's at home. I erased the footage on the security camera. I'm not stupid. You know they'll fire me for this if they found out, right? So I erased it, but I made a copy because nobody was going to believe me that that good-looking woman had wild sex with me on the desk."

"Has Sherrie Drake ever been in here before?" Jamie asked.

"Yes," he answered. "A few months ago—she worked here then—after our first date. She came in here to see me, and I showed her around and how things worked. She was very interested. She wanted to know everything—which camera was here and which switch turned this camera off."

"Mr. Roberts," Jamie snapped. "You are stupid!"

"You bring that tape to me at the police station as soon as you get off work here," Detective Nelson inserted. "Don't make another copy either."

"Do you think Sherrie had something to do with the missing child?" the security guard asked.

Detective Nelson looked at Roberts for a moment and said, "She's right"—nodding at Jamie—"you are stupid! If you hear from Miss Drake, you're going to call me." He handed Roberts a business card with his number on it.

The security guard just nodded his head and took the card.

The two detectives headed back to the police station. It was 5:15 p.m. by the time they arrived, and they both went directly to

Captain Jackson's office. Detective Nelson laid the tapes down on the captain's desk and told him what had happened.

After listening very carefully to what Detective Nelson had to say, the captain asked, "Do you think all these things are related to the councilman's death?"

"Yes I do," Nelson answered.

"This case keeps getting bigger and bigger," the captain replied. "Keep me informed because the mayor calls me every night for an update."

The detectives left the office.

"Detective Bell," the captain hollered. "Would you come back in here please?" When she did, he asked, "Would you like to have dinner with me and Sarah again tonight?"

She paused for a second before saying, "I really have a lot of work to do. Maybe tomorrow. I need to go check on Officer Garrison tonight too."

"Fine, maybe tomorrow night," he replied.

She shut the door behind her, went back to her desk, and sat down. She reached for her pencil in her pencil holder and knocked the holder over onto the floor. She bent over and started picking up the holder's contents. *What's this?* Picking up the flash drive while biting her lip and nodding up and down, she put it in her purse. Later tonight she would ask Officer Garrison what it was. She finished filling out her paperwork and drove straight to the hospital. It was getting late, and visiting hours would be over soon.

When she walked into Officer Garrison's room, he was watching TV with his wife. "Are you through with that disk?" Jamie asked.

Garrison looked at his wife, who got up from her chair and said, "I know this is police work, and I should step out of here for a few minutes. I will be down in the coffee shop."

As she stepped out the door, her husband hollered out, "Bring me back a donut. Please!"

He handed Jamie the disk and said, "I didn't find anything else on there, but you can take it to the police station and the lab could cross-reference the employee list with criminal records and see if there are any matches. I don't have access to those files from here."

Jamie pulled the flash drive out of her purse and asked him to find out what was on it.

He said, "Where did you find it?"

She replied, "It was in the pencil holder on my desk. Maybe you should look at it."

He said he would but that he was a little tired now. "I'm going home in the morning," he told her.

"Are you sure you don't know where this came from?" she repeated.

He just smiled and said, "Sure, I'm sure!"

Jamie walked out into the hallway just as Mrs. Garrison was coming down the hall with a cup of coffee and a donut. Jamie waved at her as she got into the elevator and pushed the button for the first floor. She noticed something on the stop button and looked closer.

In very small print, ink running just like it had on the stop signs, the sign read, "Stop Raping Sally."

CHAPTER 6

She stepped back against the wall of the elevator and looked up at the ceiling. "I'm trying," she let out a muffled cry. She repeated the words over and over again as she cried, banging her head on the back wall of the elevator. Finally, she reached the first floor. The door opened, and she ran out of the elevator and into the parking lot. In her car, she rested her head on her steering wheel and cried some more.

Instead of going home, she decided to go back to the police station. Maybe she could catch a little sleep there, and she would avoid the stop signs that were haunting her. She felt like she was going crazy. She had to find this little girl and save her, or she may be haunted for the rest of her life.

Back at the police station, she looked around for a place to lie down. She walked by the captain's office and remembered there was a sofa in there. She opened the door, shut it behind her, turned the light off, and lay down on his couch. For some reason, she felt safe in his office. Within moments, she was asleep.

It was now morning. Jamie had just had her first decent night's sleep in weeks. The door opened, and Captain Jackson stepped into his office, where Officer Bell was asleep on his couch. He kneeled down beside her and brushed her hair out of her face.

She seemed to have forgotten where she was, and she must have been dreaming that she was at home and he was her father, brushing her hair out of her face like he'd done when she was a child. She rolled over and mumbled, "Dad, would you make me some waffles?"

"I don't know," he answered. "I forgot my waffle iron and my batter."

Startled, she sat up quickly. Then she started apologizing over and over again. "I'm sorry. I'm so sorry," she apologized. "I shouldn't be here."

"Don't worry," the captain said. "It's fine. I sleep here all the time. That couch is very comfortable. I even have a shower in my bathroom if you want to use it."

She replied, "No, no. I'm fine. I'll freshen up in the ladies' room. I should get out of here." She slipped her shoes on and told him she would see him later. She walked out of his office and immediately went to the ladies' room.

When she opened the door and looked in the mirror, she thought, *Gee, I look like hell.* She washed her face and then dug around in her purse and found a small toothbrush and toothpaste that she kept there for emergencies. After brushing her teeth, she put her makeup on and brushed her hair and put it up in a ponytail. *Well, I look a little better*, she thought.

When she came out of the bathroom, she bumped into Detective Nelson. "You're here early," he said.

She said, "I know, I just can't get this case out of my mind."

"Stay sharp," he answered. "We have a lot of work to do today."

Jamie nodded and went to her desk. She sat down and took a deep breath; Jamie had gotten her first night of good sleep.

From behind, she heard Captain Jackson's voice. "Are you okay?"

"Yes," she said. "I'm fine."

He patted her on the shoulder and said he would see her later. As he walked away, her cell phone rang.

"Hey, Jamie," Detective Garrison said. "I found something on the flash drive I think you should look at. Can you come over to my house?"

"Yes," she said. "I'll be there within the hour."

As she was leaving, she ran into Detective Nelson, who asked where she was going. She told him she had an errand to run and that she would be back shortly.

"Don't be gone all day," he said. "We have a lot of work to do."

Within fifteen minutes, Jamie arrived at Officer Garrison's apartment. He opened the door, and as soon as she was inside, he told her she needed to look at something. He said there were a lot of e-mails to someone called K. K. A. and that the exchanges referenced a code word, "chicken," which in the children's porn world meant child. "If we could find out who this K. K. A. person is, we might have found the ringleader," Garrison suggested. Our friend, Miss Drake, comes up quite frequently," he added. "I think she is the go-between. We need to find her."

At that moment, Jamie's cell phone rang, and Detective Nelson was on the other end of the line. He told her he'd just gotten a call from the security guard, Mr. Roberts, who told him that Sherrie Drake had called him, asking all kinds of questions about the police. "Drake is supposed to meet him at dark at the phone booth by the donut shop on Eighty-Second Street," Nelson said. "Go by and pick up Mr. Roberts and bring him back to the station."

When Jamie picked Roberts up, he was very agitated and nervous. He kept telling her, "I don't know what you want me to do. I'm not a police officer."

A few minutes later, they arrived at the police station. Jamie took the security guard to see Detective Nelson, and the two followed Nelson to the equipment room. When they arrived, a technician was sitting there at a desk. He had a wire and a bulletproof vest. The security guard said, "Who is that for?"

Detective Nelson replied, "It's for you."

"And you know I'm not doing that!" the security guard shouted.

Detective Nelson shoved the security guard down in the seat and told the technician to hook him up. The security guard bitched for the next five minutes about how this was not his job. "You can't make me do this."

Detective Nelson slapped him across the face and told him to shut up. "You are going to do this," he said, "or we are going to arrest you as an accessory to kidnapping. And if I can't make that stick, I can always fall back on your having illegally taped someone without her knowledge during a sexual act. I can get you six months to a year with just that. I have the tape!"

Roberts sat in silence as Nelson and the technician continued fitting him with a wire. When that was done, they put a bulletproof vest on the security guard. Detective Nelson said, "This is for your protection."

"What if they shoot me in the face?" the security guard shot back.

"Don't worry; you're no Tom Cruise. Remember!" Detective Nelson laughed sarcastically .

It was almost dark when Detective Nelson and Jamie dropped the security guard off at the orphanage so he could drive his car to the meeting. The two detectives went to the meeting site ahead of time so they could get set up and be in place to swarm in and pick up Miss Drake. "Do not make a move until I do," Detective Nelson told Jamie. She was not to come out until she saw him come out, and she should be ready for anything he said.

Jamie waited patiently. She had a very good view this time. Finally, the security guard showed up. He got out of his car and went inside the donut shop. He got a donut and a cup of coffee and sat down. He kept looking outside at the phone booth. Finally, he got up and went to the phone booth, where he stood eating his donut and drinking his coffee. After two or three minutes, a young woman walked up. From a distance, the woman didn't look like Sherrie Drake. Her hairstyle was totally different. Maybe she was wearing a wig.

Jamie couldn't hear what Roberts and the woman were saying. She would have to rely on Detective Nelson and the technician. She could see the pair talking for a few minutes; then they walked toward his car. They separated, and the woman went to the other side of the car.

Suddenly, Jamie heard a gunshot. The security guard fell to his knees, and the woman sprinted away down an alley. Jamie jumped up and sprinted after her. She was not going to let the woman get away. At the end of an alley, a car was waiting. It was running, and its back door was open. It started pulling away slowly as the woman raced toward it. Jamie was getting closer and closer to the woman, who grabbed the door of the car as it took off. Jamie dove and tackled her.

For a moment, the car was dragging them both. Then the driver of the car pulled out his gun and fired three times at the two women.

He hit the woman and she had let go. As she and Jamie rolled through the street away from the car, it sped off. Jamie lay against the curb, holding her head. She could feel blood rolling down her face. She got up to her knees, crawled toward the woman, and rolled her over. It was Sherrie. With bullet holes in her back and shoulder, Sherrie was barely alive.

Jamie lifted her head up and asked, "Sherrie, who was the driver? Is he the man we're looking for? Is he K. K. A.?"

Sherrie smiled then coughed up some blood and tried to speak. She said, "Kirk, Kimbell, Andrew." Then she coughed a little more and said another name: "Smiling Eddie."

Jamie shook her. "What does that mean?" she demanded. "Tell me, you bitch!"

Sherrie just smiled, and then her eyes rolled back in her head and she was dead. Jamie laid the woman's head down.

Detective Nelson came running over, yelling, "Are you shot? You're bleeding." Blood streamed down Jamie's face. A little woozy now, she just lay there on the ground. Detective Nelson used his radio to call for an ambulance. He shouted repeatedly into the radio, "Officer down, officer down." He knew those words would get the quickest response, and an ambulance would be out here immediately. He kneeled down beside Jamie, put his hand across her cheek, and turned her head toward him. "Did she say anything before she died?" he asked. "You have to try and tell me."

Jamie had passed out.

He put his head on her chest to listen for her heartbeat. It was beating, and he felt relief. She wasn't dying. He grabbed his radio again and shouted into it, "Where is my ambulance?" He repeated, "Where's my ambulance? Officer down!"

Then he heard the ambulance coming down the street. An unmarked police car squealed its brakes, and Police Captain Richard Jackson got out of the car. As he ran toward the two detectives, he shouted at Detective Nelson, "Is she alive?"

Detective Nelson shouted back, "Yes!"

Captain Jackson kneeled down and grabbed Jamie's hand and shouted at Detective Nelson, "She's bleeding from the head. Was she shot?"

Detective Nelson said, "I don't think so. I think she hit her head on something, but I'm not sure." He took his handkerchief and wiped the blood out of her face and then held the handkerchief on the open wound on her head until the ambulance arrived about thirty seconds later.

The ambulance pulled up right beside them. The EMTs went to work on her immediately. Checking her for wounds, they found only cuts and scrapes, along with the one large wound on her head. One of them checked the other woman who lay there beside Jamie. The woman had been shot twice and was, reportedly, dead.

The EMTs loaded Jamie onto the gurney and lifted her into the ambulance, shutting the doors behind her. The ambulance sped off.

Captain Jackson told Detective Nelson to go to hospital. "Make sure she's all right and report back to me if she found out anything!"

CHAPTER 7

When the ambulance arrived at the hospital, Officer Garrison was there waiting. He'd heard about the shooting over his police scanner. Detective Nelson arrived. Seeing Officer Garrison, he asked where Jamie was. Garrison pointed at the examination room and said the doctors were with her. Then he asked Detective Nelson what had happened.

Detective Nelson filled him in, noting that Jamie had spoken to Sherrie Drake before Drake died and suggesting that she may have gotten some information from the exchange. "I'm going to the bathroom to wash the blood off my hands and then maybe to the coffee shop," he said.

After he left, a young doctor came out of the examination room. He told Officer Garrison that Jamie was fine. She had a slight concussion, and it had taken sixteen stitches to close the cut on her head. "You can see her now."

Officer Garrison immediately went into the room. "Hey, partner," he said. "How are you feeling?"

Jamie rubbed her head and felt the bandage on it. "My head hurts!" she said.

Officer Garrison asked, "Did Drake say anything before she died?"

Jamie paused trying to remember and then said, "She smiled at me and then said four names—Kirk, Kimbell, Andrew, and then Smiling Eddie. That's all she said before she died."

"Are the first three names different people or is it one person?" he asked.

"I don't know," Jamie said. "I just don't know. I feel a little tired now. Maybe you can put those names in the computer and see what happens. I guess the drugs they gave me are starting to take effect now. I feel like I'm falling asleep." Within a few seconds, she was.

"Jamie," Officer Garrison said. He repeated her name again, but she was asleep.

Detective Nelson walked into the room and asked how she was. Officer Garrison told him what the doctor had said and that she needed some rest. When Nelson asked Officer Garrison if Jamie had said anything about what happened or whether Miss Drake had said anything, Officer Garrison replied, "She mumbled a few things, but I couldn't understand her. And then she fell asleep."

"Keep me informed," Detective Nelson said. "I have a lot of paperwork to fill out. I'm going back to the police station."

As he left the room, Officer Garrison was thinking that maybe he should have told Detective Nelson about what Jamie had said, but he wanted to investigate the names Jamie had given him first. Maybe he could find something on his own. After all, he was all about advancement, and he knew that being able to help solve this case would be good for his career.

So he went into the waiting room. He always carried his laptop with him. At first, he went to the councilman's files that he had copied from the flash drive. Just the three letters K.K.A. of the first names came up quite often, but nothing in the files gave him a clue as to who they were.

He decided to run the names through the police computer. Before he went, he tried to access the computer from his laptop with the code word the lab techs had given him the last time he was accessing at the station. He hoped they had not changed the code word today, which they usually did every other day. He put the code word into this computer, and it worked. He had access to all the police files that were on the computer.

He plugged in the names he had to see if anything came up. The names were quite common, but none of the people's names seemed to lead to anything relating to this case. So he crossed-matched the names to sex offender registry involving children. One name came up that caught his attention—Edward Grins. Mr. Grins was both a suspected child molester and a former pharmacist who had been arrested for selling rohypnol illegally. Also, he was highly skilled in making tasers and he had been let out of prison a year and a half ago. *Could this be Smiling Eddie?* he wondered. Officer Garrison then made a mental note to himself to make copies of the mug shot of smiling Eddie.

Garrison went back to the councilman's computer files and ran a search for the name. His computer went haywire, flashing all about. It pulled up a porn site with a number to call and instructions to ask for Smiling Eddie.

Officer Garrison was so entrenched in his computer he didn't notice someone was standing behind him until Captain Richard Jackson cleared his throat and said, "Officer Garrison, what are you looking at?"

Garrison quickly closed his laptop and said, "Nothing. I was doing some research on a name."

Captain Jackson took the laptop from Officer Garrison, opened it up, and within a few minutes, he asked, "Officer Garrison, where did you get the councilman's files? Did you make a copy of the files on his laptop? You know our experts have already checked these files out."

"I know," Garrison said, "but I found something—something that might help the case. The name Edward Grins sent me to a secret porn site that was hidden in the computer, and the name 'Smiling Eddie' came up. I think it's a code word."

"That's good work," Captain Jackson said. "I think you really may have found something excellent that could break this case wide open." He pulled the flash drive out of the laptop and said, "I will personally take this to our computer technicians, and I will have them contact you as to how to access those secret files." Then he said, "Did you see Detective Bell yet? Is she okay?"

Officer Garrison, who was now beaming with confidence, said, "Yes, she's fine."

"Keep an eye on her and report back to me if there are any problems," the captain said. "And when are you going back to work?"

"As soon as the doctor releases me," Garrison said. "That's why I've been doing this computer stuff for Detective Bell, so I can stay involved in the case."

The captain patted him on the back and left. Garrison went to Jamie's room and checked on her again. She was still asleep, so he went back into the waiting room and did more work on his computer.

An hour later, Jamie woke up. When the doctor went in to check on her and saw that she was awake, he told her that everything was fine and that she could go home if she wanted to. "You have a police officer waiting for you in the waiting room. Would you like me to go get him?"

She just nodded, and a few moments later, in walked Officer Garrison. He quickly told her about what he had found with the names she had given him and how the captain had praised him for his work and how the other computer technicians would be asking him questions.

"Did you not find anything on the other three names?" she pressed.

"No," he replied. "I was still working on that. The doctor called me in to see you and said you could go home. Would you like to come to my house and stay the night? Maybe we can work a little bit on the case if you feel like it."

Jamie thought for a moment and said, "Okay, maybe that's a good idea. I really don't want to go to my house alone. Are you sure your wife won't mind?"

He answered, "I think she would be thrilled to have another woman to talk to. I'm not the best communicator in the world."

So they checked her out of the hospital, walked to his car, and drove to his house. Garrison's wife opened the front door. She told them she had made dinner and that they should go ahead, sit down and eat.

Jamie sat down and looked at the meal—lasagna with garlic bread and a banana nut cake for dessert, and everything was made from scratch. Jamie was excited about getting a home-cooked meal. She didn't cook much and ate out most of the time.

When the meal was over, Jamie thanked Mrs. Garrison for the meal. She told Jamie to call her Amy, that Dan's mother was Mrs. Garrison.

Jamie helped Amy clear the dishes and wash them, and the women talked while cleaning up. Amy thanked Jamie for saving her husband's life. She almost started to cry but held it in. Then she told her how much she loved Dan.

"I like him too," Jamie responded. "I think he's a great partner and computer geek."

After the dishes were done, Jamie and Dan started working on the computer again. They kept searching the police files for those three names, trying to find any link they could to their case.

After hours of searching, Officer Garrison came up with an idea. He said, "Maybe those names are a code name, like Smiling Eddie was a code name for Edward Grins.

Jamie asked, "You mean like the name Kirk is a code name for something else?"

He said, "Yes. Maybe the letters mean something more or they're out of order. Or maybe they're initials for someone's name."

"My head is hurting," Jamie said, rubbing it. "Trying to figure out what those names mean could take months. We don't have that kind of time."

"I will go into my computer and try and come up with some kind of list," Garrison said. "Maybe if I print out the names something will ring a bell."

The next morning, Jamie woke early. She had decided to take a quick shower and go to the police station early. She felt uncomfortable at Garrison's house, so she needed to get out of there. As she started to leave, Amy came into the room and asked if everything was all right. Jamie said that everything was fine. "I just feel like I need to go by my house and into the police station," she explained. "I'm fine. Don't worry. Tell Dan I will call him later. And it was nice to get to know you better, Amy." She said good-bye as she closed the door.

In her car, she drove straight to the station. When she arrived, she walked toward her desk. She could see her chair moving back and forth slowly. She moved toward her chair and spun it around. To her surprise, Sarah was sitting in her chair.

The little girl giggled and said, "Where you been, Jingle Bells?" Jamie couldn't help but laugh.

Sarah continued, "You have a bandage on your head. Does it hurt?"

Jamie answered, "Yes, it hurts."

Captain Jackson came out of the restroom then and he asked Sarah if she was ready to go to school. Then he asked Jamie if she was okay. Jamie told him she was fine.

Then little Sarah turned to Jamie. "Would you come to my Christmas pageant?" she asked.

Jamie looked at Captain Jackson and said, "When is it?"

"It's next week," he answered. "But you don't have to come."

"Well, I think I would like to go," Jamie replied. "Yes, Sarah, I would love to go to your Christmas pageant. You tell me what day and what time, and I will be there."

Sarah jumped out of Jamie's chair and hugged her tightly.

Captain Jackson grabbed Sarah by the hand and said, "Come on now; we have to get you to school."

As they walked away, little Sarah waved at Jamie and started singing "Jingle Bells" again.

Jamie pored over the evidence they had. It wasn't much, but there was one common place—the donut shop. She decided to sit there for a while. Maybe she'd show the picture of Edward Grins that Officer Garrison had given her to the people who worked there.

At the donut shop, she ordered a couple of donuts and a diet soda and sat down. She stared out the window and just watched, looking for anything. After an hour or so, a young man from behind the counter approached her and started cleaning up the nearby tables.

She couldn't help but notice him. He was rather good-looking and a little cocky. He asked her if she needed a refill on her drink and then flashed his beautiful smile.

"Sure," she said.

He picked up her drink, went over to the machine, and refilled it. Then he blurted out his cheesy opening line. "I haven't seen you around here before. See anything you like?" He pointed toward himself.

Maybe, she thought to herself as she smiled at him. *I could use him, flirt with him a little bit, make him think he has a chance with me, and get him to do a little detective work for me.*

She asked him to sit down and showed him the picture of the man she was looking for. She made up a story about the man, saying she was working for a long-lost relative and she was searching for him, as he'd inherited a lot of money.

The young man took the picture and looked at it closely. "Yeah," he said after a moment. "I've seen this dude before. He's been in here a couple of times." He handed the picture back to Jamie.

"I need to find him," she said. "There's a big commission in this for me. But if he finds out that his family is looking for him, he'll run. They had a bad falling out, so you can't tell him I'm looking for him. Just let me know when he's here. Or maybe you could strike up a friendship with him and maybe get a phone number or address. Just be your charming self, the way you were with me, and I will compensate you."

The young man looked at Jamie and said, "Compensation? I wasn't really looking for any compensation. But if that's what you want to call it, that's fine with me," he added with a wink.

She pulled a napkin out of the napkin holder, took out her pen, and wrote down her cell phone number and her first name. When she extended here hand, he shook it and then pulled it toward his mouth and kissed it. "My name is Sam," he said.

Someone shouted from the back, "Sam, get back to work! Quit flirting with the customers."

Sam rubbed Jamie's hand before leaping back over the counter. He was quite athletic.

Jamie stayed another fifteen or twenty minutes. Then she decided to go to the councilman's wife's house and show her the picture. Maybe she had seen Edward Grins and had some information.

When the councilman's wife answered the door, she seemed excited to see Jamie. She was feeling like the investigation was going nowhere and the killer of her husband would never be found. Jamie caught her up on the details of the ongoing investigation—at least the details she could share our of her husband's death; she explained that she and the other detectives were following several leads and said she was sure that one of them would lead to her husband's killer.

Then she handed the councilman's wife a picture of Edward Grins. "Have you ever seen this man before?" she asked.

The councilman's wife studied the picture for a few seconds and then she said, "Yes. I've seen this man several times at my husband's office. But I don't recognize the name."

Jamie asked her, "Did he call himself Kirk, Kimball, or Andrew?"

As the councilman's wife handed the picture back to Jamie, she said, "No, but I do recall my husband calling him Eddie once."

"Could it have been Smiling Eddie?" Jamie asked.

"Yes, that's it. That was what he called him! I asked him once who the man was. He just said a friend of a friend's and left it at that."

"Did your husband ever hang out at a donut shop?"

"As a matter of fact, he did. I don't know which one it was, but he would say he was going out for a donut—all the time."

Jamie told the councilman's wife that she'd been most helpful. "I will keep you informed," she added.

Back in her car, Jamie mulled over the new information she had and thought about the councilman's wife. She seemed so lovely and innocent. She had no idea that her husband had been involved in some kind of kiddie porn ring. This would be devastating to her, and Jamie didn't want to be the one who had to tell her.

Before driving home, Jamie checked her cell phone for messages. Both the captain and Detective Nelson had called to check on her. But she wasn't okay. She was very frustrated with this case. She felt like a little girl's life was in danger, and she was no closer to finding the little girl or the councilman's killer. She stared at the photo again. "It has to be you," she whispered.

She drove home, and there again, two blocks from her house was a stop sign with the message: "Stop Raping Sally!" In her frustration, Jamie punched her accelerator to the floor and rolled over the stop sign. She continued on to the next stop sign, a block before her house, which carried the same message. She drove over it, crashing it to the ground. *If you destroy the signs*, she reasoned with herself, *maybe they will stop haunting you and the city will come out and replace them with new signs.*

Inside the house, Jamie called the station. She made up an excuse, saying she wasn't feeling well and that she wanted to lie down and take a nap. She said she would be back tomorrow. She made herself a sandwich and then took one of the tranquilizers the doctor had given her to help her sleep. Within a few minutes, she was asleep.

She sat up in her bed in the middle of the night and looked at her clock. It was 3:00 a.m. She had been asleep for almost eleven hours. She heard a banging outside her front picture window, so she timidly walked to the window opened her drapes to see what was going on. She screamed in horror. Then she saw what was there: the two stop signs were banging against her house, displaying their messages prominently: "Stop Raping Sally!"

She ran back to her bedroom. Sitting in the corner, she pulled her comforter over her head and clutched her pistol. The banging grew louder and louder.

"Stop!" she screamed at the top of her lungs. "Please stop!"

CHAPTER 8

Jamie must have fallen back into a deep sleep because the sunlight peaking through the window woke her in the morning. She pulled her comforter off of herself and walked over to the window and opened the drapes. The stop signs were no longer there. She put her robe on and ran down to the end of the block. There the stop signs lay. She walked back to her house, thinking, *I drove over the stop signs. That must've got into my subconscious somehow. Or maybe it was a reaction from the concussion.* Or she was going crazy?

Even thought it was very early in the morning, she decided to get ready and go into work. Officer Garrison was supposed to be in today, since his doctor released him, giving him light-duty status. It had started to rain again as she drove into work. She noticed the other stop sign that she had knocked down.

When she arrived at work, Detective Nelson and Captain Jackson were waiting for her at her desk. The captain said, "I heard you went over to the donut shop on your way home last night and were asking some questions. Did you get any answers?"

She was puzzled. How did the captain know where she'd been?

Detective Nelson said, "I must have just missed you because the owner told me a pretty girl came in asking questions, and the description he and the kid behind the counter gave of the woman made me think it was you."

Jamie just stood there with her mouth open as the captain chastised her for working alone. "We have had two people killed, and two officers were injured in that neighborhood in the last week. You cannot go out on your own in that neighborhood anymore! Do you understand?" he said sternly.

She just stood there and nodded her head. She bit her lip to keep herself from speaking, folded her arms, and looked up toward the ceiling.

The captain continued, "I have to take Sarah to school now. Detective Nelson, fill Detective Bell in on what you're going to do today." He walked down the hall, picked up his daughter, and headed out the door.

Detective Nelson told Jamie to sit down. "Look," he said. "I admire your enthusiasm, but this has become a very dangerous case. Someone is killing suspects and they already tried to kill your partner and you. The captain is just concerned about your safety. Just wait here until Officer Garrison gets here. We'll map out our strategy for today." He walked away toward the break room to get a cup of coffee.

Jamie just sat at her desk staring at a blank computer screen. She was mad; she felt like Captain Jackson and Detective Nelson were handcuffing her on this investigation.

A few moments later, Officer Garrison walked in. "Jamie, what's wrong?" he asked. "You look like somebody ran over your dog."

"The captain just balled me out for doing my job," she responded.

Officer Garrison had a dumb look on his face.

"Just forget about it," she said. "I'll fill you in later. We are supposed to sit here until Detective Nelson comes back and gives us something to do."

Officer Garrison handed her a piece of paper. It was a printout from his computer—a list of names. There must have been twenty to thirty names on the paper.

"What's this?" she asked.

"This," he answered, "is a list of names that have something in common with the three names you gave me. The way I went on this might be a little radical, but when I'm sitting at home with nothing else to do, I kind of go a little crazy."

As Jamie studied the list, Detective Nelson came running over, carrying two bulletproof vests and two shotguns. He shouted at Jamie, "Get another uniformed officer and come with me."

As Jamie and Garrison chased Nelson down the hallway toward the exit, Jamie grabbed the first officer who walked by and told him to come with her. Detective Nelson was standing in front of his car loading the shotguns.

When the others arrived, he told them that Captain Jackson had just called and given him the location of a possible suspect—Edward Grins. "We are going to go in quietly and try and catch him by surprise," Detective Nelson explained. "No sirens."

He didn't speak again until they got about a block from the house. Then he turned to the others and said, "I will go in the front door. Officer Garrison, you will back me up." He pointed to the other officer and Jamie, "You two will go to the back. I want you to just cover the back door. Do not come in. Anybody who comes out of the back door—if they're armed—you tell them to drop the weapon. If they do not, shoot to kill. Take no chances.

Remember, he could have a small child with him. Don't make a mistake!"

Jamie and the uniformed officer crept up to the door at the back of the house, and soon everyone had gotten into position.

Detective Nelson whispered into his radio, "Okay, I'm going in." He kicked down the door. With a shotgun pointed directly into the house, he scanned the room from side to side. He walked quietly through the house, searching for movement.

He came to a shut door that presumably led to a bedroom door. Sensing something was on the other side, he took precautions. He kicked the door and stepped out of the way. Then he got down and peeked around the door. He could see a bed. All of a sudden, he heard a rustling sound. Something was moving across the floor. He rolled into the room with a shotgun raised and ready to fire.

It was rats, just rats, rustling through the trash. McDonald's wrappers and empty boxes of donuts littered the room, but nobody was there.

Detective Nelson walked to the back of the house and out the back door. He waved for Jamie and the other officer to come inside. Back at the front door, he waved Officer Garrison in too. When they all were inside, he told them, "We must have missed them, but someone has been here. Let's give this house the once-over. Be very careful not to disturb anything. Put your gloves on, search for clues, and if you think you find something, holler out to me."

They all took a different room, being very careful not to disturb anything. After about five minutes, the young police officer hollered out. He had found two or three paper sacks. As he opened each one, he could see hair inside. Detective Nelson came over. He carefully opened one of the sacks. Inside was an Afro wig and dark brown tanning cream. The other sack had a blonde wig in it.

The wigs were small, Jamie thought, children's size. "He was here, I know it; I just know it!" she said.

Officer Garrison yelled out, "Come here, come here now!"

They all ran over to him. With his gun pointed down at a door, he said to Detective Nelson, "There's a basement."

Detective Nelson said, "I will go in first. Don't shoot me in the back."

He signaled to Officer Garrison to open the door. Detective Nelson raised his shotgun, pulled out his flashlight, and walked downstairs. It was very dark, and the stairs creaked all the way down. When Detective Nelson reached the bottom, he saw a very nice bed, a generator, and a videotaping camera all set up and ready to record. There were freestanding fluorescent lights, still warm to the touch. Detective Nelson set his flashlight down, took a handkerchief out of his pocket, and turned on the lights. Glass containers filled with powders of various colors and consistencies lay on a table near the bed, along with a pill-making machine, and a notepad. The first page of the notepad listed several pharmaceutical-sounding names, most of which had been scratched out. One of the names—baby roofies—had been circled. Three Tasers also lay on the table; one of them was torn apart, as if it was being worked on.

Jamie looked inside the video camera. There was no tape.

Detective Nelson felt the generator. It was hot. He yelled out, "Damn it, we just missed them!"

As Jamie walked around the basement, she could hear the wind whistling. The house was very old and abandoned. A cardboard box lay against the wall. A funny smell drew Jamie toward it. She knelt down beside it and pressed her ear against the box. To her surprise she heard a panting sound, or breathing, and her instincts told her it was the child. Hurriedly she pulled it away from the wall, and all Jamie could see were teeth coming at her and a large pit bull pounced on her, missing her throat by inches. The dog snarled and barked. Jamie's hands were all that held the pit bull back from biting her in the face.

Detective Nelson blew the dog's head off with his shotgun. The animal lay bleeding on top of Jamie. As she pushed it off, Detective Nelson helped her up. She wiped her face. She was really angry now. There was no stopping her.

She noticed light coming through a broken window and crawled outside through the window. She saw a small, muddy handprint on the ground—a child's handprint. It led to an alleyway that was covered with trees and brush. As she followed the path through the brush, she saw tiny footprints and large footprints and more handprints. It looked like an adult and a child had crawled through the brush. The passageway was about thirty yards from the house. There was no way you could see anyone crawling on it from either the road in front of the house or the back of the house. Whoever left these prints could've been there the whole time.

Jamie reached the alleyway; it was gravel. They could have run either way.

When Detective Nelson reached her, he said, "They were here. Are you all right?"

She turned to him. "The child must be frightened out of her mind," she said. "And for that dog to sit there quietly and wait till that box was moved before it attacked. It had to be well trained."

Detective Nelson agreed. "Son of a bitch," he said, kicking the gravel. "This is all my fault. If I would have waited another thirty minutes, we would have had more police officers and maybe we could've caught them." He radioed for a print team, instructing the team to fingerprint the whole house.

Detective Nelson dreaded going back to the station. He knew that Captain Jackson was going to chew his ass out over this screw up. They waited for the team to arrive; then they all went back to the station. Detective Nelson told Jamie and Officer Garrison to fill out their reports of what had happened and said that he would go talk to Captain Jackson. He went into the captain's office and shut the door.

Jamie could hear Captain Jackson yelling at him even at her desk. She went to the restroom to clean the rest of the blood off of her face and change her shirt. When she looked in the mirror, she could see blood from the dog still in her hair. *Gross!* she thought. She washed the blood out of her hair the best she could, put her hair in a ponytail, and went to her desk and pulled out a baseball cap and put it on.

Officer Garrison came over to her and asked her if she had looked over the list he had given her.

She looked at him very puzzled and said, "You know I haven't. I was cleaning the blood out of my hair and changing my shirt."

"We really need to look over this," he said. "I know the answer is here. And I found one more bit of information that might be meaningless, but it was too big a coincidence for me not to ask you about it. Do you remember the guy you shot in the nightclub?"

"Yes," she said.

"His name was Johnny Tate. He was a cellmate of Edward Grins one year ago. They were together about six months."

Jamie looked at Officer Garrison and said, "Do you see a connection here with the nightclub shooting and all of this stuff?"

He shrugged his shoulders and said, "I don't know. It just seemed a bit odd to me."

Jamie sat down at her desk and pulled out the file on Johnny Tate. She was looking for anything that would connect him with this other case. According to the file, he was a small-time criminal with a bad drug habit. He had been in and out of jail and placed in drug treatment programs several times. As she started to read the arrest reports, Captain Jackson yelled at Jamie to get into his office. She lay the file down and handed it to Officer Garrison. "Look at this. Maybe you can see something here," she said before she walked into the captain's office.

The first thing out of his mouth was, "Are you okay?"

She said she was fine. "It could've been a lot worse if Detective Nelson hadn't acted so rapidly. The dog was going for my throat, and I couldn't have stopped that from happening if Detective Nelson had not shot the dog. You shouldn't yell at him. We were all at fault; that exit from the house was hidden. I don't think more police officers would have made much difference."

The captain looked at her. "Maybe you're right," he said, "but from now on, I want you to keep me informed. Anytime you think Detective Nelson is doing his Lone Ranger impersonation, he is putting young officers at risk, and I don't like that! The captain leaned forward from his desk. His eyes were filled with compassion when he said, "Do you need to go home? Are you okay?"

"I'm fine," she answered.

"Well, go back to work!" he replied.

Jamie walked back to her desk, trying to remember what she was doing. She started to look for the Johnny Tate file, but she remembered she'd handed it to Officer Garrison. She picked up the photo of Johnny Tate and said to herself, *I need a diet soda and a donut*. She was going back to the donut shop and she would show Tate's photo to the handsome young man who worked there. On the way out of the station, she asked Officer Garrison if he wanted a donut and said she should be back in about an hour.

"Yes, one with chocolate sprinkles," he replied.

She drove to the donut shop, hoping to see the handsome young man. Once she arrived, she sat in her car watching the counter. Finally, Sam arrived, taking the back entrance into the shop and taking over the register for the other man who'd been working. Jamie got out of her car and went to the door.

As she walked in, Sam yelled out, "What can I get you, beautiful? Would you like regular donuts or a long john? I have both!" He laughed.

She ordered her drink and donut and sat down at a table by the window, off by herself, waiting for Sam to bring them to her. When he brought her order over, she asked him to sit down. He was very cocky and sure of himself. He assumed she was coming there to see him.

"What can I do for you, beautiful?" he asked.

She showed him the picture of Johnny Tate and asked if he'd ever seen the man here before.

Sam looked the picture over very closely and said, "Yes. He has been here before, but it's been a while. I haven't seen him in several weeks."

"Well that's because he's dead," Jamie said. She then showed him a picture of Edward Grins. She asked, "Do you remember this guy?"

He said he did. "That's the dude you're looking for. They used to come in here together."

Jamie asked, "Are you sure?"

"Yes, I'm positive," he said. "What's with all the questions? I thought you came in here to see me," he added playfully.

"He hasn't been back here?" She pointed to the picture of Edward Grins.

He smiled again and rocked back in his chair. "I told you I would call you if I seen him. He hasn't been in, and believe me, I would've called just to get another look at you, beautiful."

Jamie stood up, grabbed her diet soda and bag of donuts, and told the handsome young man she had to go back to work. "But you call me if you see this man, and we'll get together. I promise."

Sam hopped back over the counter and patted his boss on the shoulder as Jamie walked out the door. He said, "Just look at her ass. It won't be long until that ass is in my apartment.

On the drive back to the station, Jamie thinking to herself, *Everything is connected somehow.*

Back at the police station, she told Officer Garrison what she had found out. The rest of the day went by slowly. Jamie and Garrison still couldn't figure out what the connection was.

Five o'clock rolled around, and it was time to go home. Officer Garrison told her they could start fresh tomorrow, that maybe something new would turn up. Jamie just sat at her desk with her hands folded on the back of her head and stared at a blank computer screen.

She was still there at almost six o'clock when, suddenly, two little hands covered Jamie's eyes. "Guess who?" a small voice said.

Jamie said, "Is it Santa Claus?"

The little girl said, "No."

Jamie guessed again and said, "Is it Rudolph the Red-nosed Reindeer?"

The little girl laughed and said, "No."

Jamie spun her chair around and said, "It must be Sarah." She hugged the little girl.

Sarah asked Jamie, "We are going to eat, and then we're going to a movie. Would you like to come?"

Jamie paused for half a second and answered quickly, "Yes." With all of the stress that she had been put through lately, a meal with a happy little girl and a movie sounded like the perfect medicine. Sarah then took Jamie by the hand and pulled her to her dad's office. He was just now getting off the phone.

Captain Jackson asked his daughter, "Did you ask her?"

"Yes," Sarah said.

"Well," he answered, "what did she say?"

Jamie looked at her captain and said, "I would love to eat. Let's go."

While driving toward McDonald's, little Sarah was in the backseat, trying to stretch her fingers out.

Jamie asked her, "What are you doing?"

She pointed her fingers toward Jamie, spread apart, and said, "Peace. Live long and prosper."

Jamie looked awfully puzzled. She looked at her captain and said, "What does that mean?"

He just shook his head and said, "Haven't you ever watched the old TV series *Star Trek*?"

"No," Jamie said. "Maybe a little when I was a kid."

"We watch it all the time," he said. "I have it on DVD. Sarah's favorite character is Spock."

Sarah then blurted out, "And my daddy's favorite character is Captain James T. Kirk of the Starship *Enterprise*." For the next couple of minutes Sarah rambled on and on about the TV show. She knew all the characters by name.

"She has quite an imagination," Jamie told the captain. "I've never seen any little girl know that much about a TV show, other than *Barney* or *Sesame Street*."

When they arrived at McDonald's and sat down to eat, Jamie asked, "What movie are we seeing?"

"It's some animated TV movie that's out now," he replied. "I can't remember."

Sarah blurted out the title over and over again.

Her dad replied, "Oh, that's it."

Jamie asked Sarah, "What is your favorite movie?"

Sarah answered, "*Old Yeller.* I cry every time he dies." She asked Jamie what her favorite movie was.

Jamie thought about it for a minute and then said, "I think my favorite movie is *Old Yeller* too, and I cry every time a dog dies." Jamie and Sarah giggled together. Then Jamie asked her captain what his favorite movie was.

He answered very quickly, without hesitation, "I love all Harrison Ford movies. I think my favorite is *The Fugitive.* I like how he outsmarts the police throughout the movie. He should've won an Oscar for playing the part of Dr. Richard Kimble."

The meal was soon over and the trio drove to the movie theater. They purchased their tickets and waited in line for popcorn for little Sarah, and of course she had to have candy. They watched the movie, which lasted an hour and a half. Sarah thoroughly enjoyed herself. She was a happy little girl. She sang the songs in the movie and laughed at all the jokes.

While they were leaving the movie theater, little Sarah begged her father to buy her a stuffed animal of the lead character in the movie. As he pulled his money out of his wallet a twenty-dollar bill fell on the floor. Sarah picked it up and pointed to the picture on the bill. She said to Jamie, "This man is related to my father."

With a puzzled look on her face, Jamie looked at Richard and said, "Is that true?"

"Yes," he replied, "my great-great-grandfather was his cousin. So I'm related to President Andrew Jackson. How's that for a family tree?"

Jamie responded, "I'm impressed."

They left the movie theater and headed back to the station so Jamie could get her car. There was something different about this drive back to the station. It was silent. Little Sarah had fallen asleep in her car seat. Richard pulled into the parking lot and turned off the motor. He thanked Jamie again for going. He told her how hard it had been for Sarah and himself since his wife was killed. He said it was easier for him if she fell asleep in the car and he carried her up to bed because when he tucked her in at night, that's when she missed her mother the most. He went on and on, talking about their lives. A single tear rolled down his face when he talked about his wife.

This was a side of the captain Jamie hadn't seen very often. As she sat there and listened to him pour his heart out, a sudden urge came over her. She pulled him close and hugged him.

He looked into her eyes and kissed her ever so gently. He pulled away and said, "I shouldn't have done that. I'm sorry!"

Jamie responded, "No. It's okay. I wanted it too. It felt good. It felt right."

Before Jamie could get out of the car, Sarah woke up screaming! "Mommy, Mommy, help me!" She was kicking and screaming and yelling, "That hurts."

Jamie stood there in horror, listening to the fear and the little girl's voice Sarah ramble on and on. Captain Jackson reached back to his daughter and shook her, trying to calm her down. Sarah tried reaching for Jamie; her little eyes were filled with tears. As Jamie climbed into the back seat she sat there and hugged her and let the little girl cry in her arms.

The captain said in a stern voice, "She will be all right. She has these nightmares every once in a while about her mother."

Jamie rubbed the back of Sarah's head. As Sarah tried to hang on, Jamie pulled away to get out of the car. Jamie got out of the car and said, "I will see you tomorrow, Richard," Jamie was still shaken by the child's outburst. She tried to wave at Sarah without showing any emotion. The captain nodded and waved as he drove off.

Jamie walked into the police station to use the restroom. When she'd exited the building and made her way back to her car, she saw a figure near it; it seemed that an old wino was sleeping right next to her car. "Hey, buddy, you're going to have to move," she said to the bum. "Find somebody else's car sleep on."

The bum moaned and said something as he staggered to his feet. She couldn't understand a word he said. He started to walk away but turned and grabbed her. He pushed her to the car and got right in her face, shouting at her, "Stop raping Sally. You must stop him!" He repeated it again. "Stop raping Sally!" He then shoved her to the ground.

Chapter 9

Jamie pulled out her weapon, and with blinding speed the dirty old bum ran off. He weaved in and out of the parked cars like a jungle cat. She just sat there and watched him vanish into the night. She got up and put her gun back in her holster and then opened her car and got inside. She locked her door and started her car. Reluctantly, she drove home. With all this spooky stuff that was happening to her, being home alone was the last thing she wanted.

She was happy to see no stop signs with the words "Stop Raping Sally" on them. She went inside, locked the door, and checked all the windows. She went to her refrigerator and opened up a can of diet soda. Rummaging through her medicine cabinet, she found a bottle of tranquilizers and took two. She didn't even undress. She turned the TV on, grabbed a blanket, and lay on the couch, hoping she would pass out soon. Within moments, she was asleep.

The next morning, Jamie awoke to her alarm going off in the bedroom. The tranquilizers had worked. She'd slept all night.

While she was getting ready for work, her doorbell rang. Her first instinct was to grab her gun and quietly walk to the door. She peeked out the window. Officer Garrison was standing on the porch. He started to knock on the door, and when she opened it, she asked him what he was doing. He told her he was worried about her. He said he'd tried to call her several times last night, but she hadn't answered her phone and it had gone straight to voice mail.

"I went to a movie last night," she told him. "I felt I needed to get away from the case."

"By yourself?" he asked.

"No. I went with the captain and his daughter."

A puzzled look crossed Garrison's face. "You seem to spend an awful lot of time with the captain. Are you dating him or something?" he asked.

She replied, "No, I'm not dating him. He is going through a tough time with the death of his wife, and his daughter has somehow latched herself onto me."

Officer Garrison told Jamie that he felt she was ignoring his theory on the case. She hadn't even looked at the list of names he'd given her the other day. "And if we work together on this, we can solve this case. Why didn't you tell me about your conversation at the donut shop with the young guy!"

"Look," she said. "I was grasping at straws. The guy was flirting with me. I thought maybe I could use him to get some information. And if he came through, no harm no foul."

Officer Garrison asked, "What did he say?"

"I showed him a few pictures of the guys we were looking for, and I told him to call me or text me if and when they showed up here. And I admit that I flirted with the guy." She added, "I would even sleep with the guy if I thought I could solve this case. That's how dedicated I am to this case!"

"Would you like to come over to my house for dinner tonight?" Garrison asked. "We could go over the list tonight."

"I can't tonight," she answered. "I promised a little girl I would go to her Christmas pageant. We can go over it tomorrow. Detective

Nelson and I have to go downtown to redo some interviews. It should take most of the day. I'm sorry I haven't kept you informed on every aspect of the case, but now that the captain has taken you off desk duty, we can work closely again. We will go over all of your theories tomorrow, but I can't get out of these interviews today. Just go over all of my notes on the case, and we can pick it up again tomorrow."

Garrison still wasn't satisfied. Maybe she thought she was protecting him that he would be a good police officer and just accept what his superior officer was telling him. As he left her house, he told her he would call her if he came up with anything new. He went back to the precinct.

Later that afternoon, the captain called Officer Garrison into his office and asked him about the list. He had made up some kind of code. Officer Garrison explained his theory to the captain. "The names—Kirk, Kimble, Jackson—show up quite often in the computer files. I think our computer techs were going the wrong way. Instead of looking for those names in the pedophile database, I think these names are codes—that Kirk stands for something else. I'm going way out on a limb here. When I say it could be as simple as Douglas or any other famous Kirk. Do you get where I'm going, sir?" While he did so, little Sarah and her nanny arrived at the captain's office.

Sarah was carrying a DVD player and what appeared to be a case of movies. She tripped over Officer Garrison's foot, and her case of movies fell onto the floor, scattering everywhere. He quickly helped her up and then picked up the DVDs and put them back into her carrying case. He couldn't help but notice some of the DVD titles—*Star Trek*, *Indiana Jones*, *The Fugitive*, and of course, *Old Yeller*.

Garrison said to Sarah, "Those are some real good movies."

"*Star Trek* is my all-time favorite."

The captain told Officer Garrison to keep him informed if he thought he'd broken the code, assuming there was one. "I have to get ready for Sarah's Christmas pageant. We have to be there early."

Officer Garrison returned to his desk, pulled out his list, and started going over it again. He thought of a couple more names that could be added. It was getting late, so he decided to go home. Maybe he would work on the list a little later.

Jamie arrived at the station. She was running late from the interviews and would have to hurry to get to the Christmas pageant before it started. She drove straight to Sarah's school. When she walked into the auditorium she searched the crowd for Captain Jackson. He was supposed to save her a seat. Finally she saw him waving at her. Before she walked down the aisle, her cell phone rang. She could see it was Officer Garrison calling her. She quickly turned her cell phone to silent. She would call him back later, after the pageant. She put her cell phone inside her jacket pocket and quickly walked down the aisle, taking her jacket off, laying it in her seat, and sitting down next to Captain Jackson. They exchanged pleasantries.

Then the auditorium lights were turned down. The pageant had started. The school choir sang several Christmas songs. Jamie asked Captain Jackson when Sarah would be on. He told her she had a small part in the play. After intermission Jamie excused herself. She had to go the restroom and told him she would be right back.

While she was gone, a tone alerting her that a text message had come in went off. The captain curiously looked inside her jacket and pulled out her phone. He read the text message and then put the phone back.

A lot of other women must have had the same idea because there was a line waiting outside the restroom. After about five minutes, finally, it was Jamie's turn to use the restroom. Intermission was nearly over when she arrived back at her seat. Jackson told her it was his turn to go, and he would hurry before the pageant started. She sat down, and the text message tone went off on her phone. She had received a text message from Sam. He had some information for her on the guy she was looking for, but he would only give it to her in person. She needed to meet him at the donut shop at 9:00 p.m. She looked at the time on her cell phone. It was 8:00 p.m. Her first thought was to tell the captain, but she didn't know how reliable the information would be, so she would make an excuse to leave after Sarah's performance and before the pageant was over. She could always call the captain after she'd talked to Sam.

The captain returned and sat down beside her. The play was just now starting. After fifteen minutes, Sarah appeared. She was so cute in her Christmas costume. She said her lines flawlessly. You could see her looking out into the crowd, searching for her dad, and her eyes brightened up when she saw Jamie sitting beside him. She couldn't help but wave at them as she was leaving the stage.

When the play was over, there was a grand finale, where all the kids in the play all came out to sing. Jamie looked at her cell phone. She had just enough time to meet Sam at the donut shop if she left right now. She told the captain she had an appointment at nine o'clock that she could not miss.

He told her that Sarah would be disappointed. "I told her we would go out to dinner after the pageant."

Jamie just made her apologies and told him she would call them later. "This is very important. I must go."

While driving to the donut shop, she called Officer Garrison's cell phone, but there was no answer. She thought she'd try him back after she talked to Sam.

Sam, apparently off duty, was waiting outside the donut shop. She walked up to him and said, "Well, what do you have?"

He handed her a piece of paper and said, "On this piece of paper are the address and directions to where this scumbag lives. He was there about an hour ago. I followed him to the address on the piece of paper. Now, when are we going out? You owe me big-time for following this guy into that bad of a neighborhood. I felt like I had to take a shower, just walking through the neighborhood, and if I were you, I wouldn't go alone."

She smiled at him and said, "Thanks for the information. We can go out if you want to, but you're really not my type." She giggled and said, "I like women, but I do owe you something." She walked up to him, pulled him close, and gave him a big kiss on the mouth. She then let go.

He looked into her eyes and said, "What a waste." He shook his head and walked away.

Jamie pulled out her cell phone and tried to call Garrison again. There was still no answer. She knew she couldn't call the captain, as he was still at the pageant, so she called Detective Nelson. Getting no answer there either, she left a voice mail, telling him the situation and that she was going to investigate alone.

When she arrived in the neighborhood Sam's directions led her to, she turned her lights off. She decided to call Captain Jackson and tell him what was going on.

When he answered, she filled him in that she had a lead an address of possible location of Edward Grins. She was only three blocks away. He told her to check the house out, "But do not go inside until I get there!"

The wind was now picking up. It was starting to rain, and a thunder and lightning storm was in the forecast. Jamie sneaked up to the house. It was very dark. A stop sign rattled in the wind on the corner by the house. She crawled up to the high grass behind the trashcans and peeked into a nearby window to see if she could see any movement in the house. It was raining and getting harder with each moment. Jamie's adrenaline was flowing. Every instinct she had told her this was the answer. She came to another window. She could see a small night-light. A mattress lay on the floor. Next to the mattress, something appeared to move. *Could it be?* she asked herself.

She looked closer, pointed her flashlight through the window, and turned it on and then quickly off. In the flash of the light, she had seen the rise and fall of a child's chest, her arms and feet appeared to be tied with ropes. The wind blew over the trashcans. Jamie saw a car coming in the distance. Its lights were off. It was Captain Jackson. Jamie flashed her flashlight toward the captain, signaling her location.

He crawled up toward the house and stopped beside Jamie. She told him that a little girl was in there but that she hadn't seen anyone else.

He whispered. "You go in the front. I will go in the back. There's no time for backup. We have to make this call right."

She nodded in agreement and crept to the front porch. She tried the doorknob, and it was locked, of course. She took a deep breath. Lightning flashed in the background behind her, and thunder roared in the wind. She kicked open the door and rolled inside with her weapon raised. She heard the back door being kicked open and saw the captain's flashlight. They checked the wide, open front room from their respective doors. Moving carefully, they arrived at the last door of a long hallway—the door to the room where Jamie had seen the little girl.

It was locked. The captain kicked the door open. A little girl, scared out her mind, tried to get to her feet. But she was tied up, and she fell back to the floor.

Jamie rushed to her side. She whispered into her ear, "Everything is fine. The police are here to help. Is there anyone else here?" Jamie asked.

The little girl shook her head no.

Jamie peeled the duct tape off the child's mouth slowly.

The captain was looking out the window. "Someone is coming," he told Jamie.

The little girl dug her fingernails into the side of Jamie's arm. She was petrified. Jamie whispered to the girl, telling her to be very still and very quiet. Jamie stood up in the doorway with her weapon raised. The captain had moved across the hall. They both had a clear sight of the front door.

A man walked through the kicked in front door with no fear. He shouted out, "Hey, Richie. Look what I found." He pulled another child out of the shadows, but Jamie couldn't see the child's face.

She looked toward the captain. Anger spread over his face, and he mouthed the word *Sally*!

Within a split second, the captain fired his gun three times into the man.

As the man fell to the ground over the little girl, Jamie rushed to help the child. In an instant, everything was clear. It was like time had stood still. While pulling Edward Grins off the child, Jamie's mind raced back to the first time she met Sarah—Sarah Ann Lavone Young. *She was going to tell me her mother calls her Sally. She was interrupted before she could tell me that.*

She turned and looked toward the captain. He glared at her, and in that instant, she knew. Jamie tried to pull her weapon, but Sally grabbed her arm. Jamie felt an electrical charge in her back. She fell to the ground, paralyzed. She had been Tasered by the captain. The charge had gone through Jamie's body and hit Sally. They both lay motionless on the floor.

The captain rolled Jamie over. "Well, you figured it out," he said. "I don't know how you knew Sarah's nickname was Sally. Maybe my wife's ghost was the one writing on all those stop signs by your house. I know you can hear me. This taser is a wondrous weapon; one little charge from this thing and you lie motionless for ten to twenty minutes. You can't move. I always have had a fetish for young girls. I'm very twisted that way. I accidentally tasered Sally, and she lay there motionless. I gave her a spoonful of one of Smiling Eddie's baby roofies—it was a liquid formula—a few months ago, and I acted out one of my fantasies on her. It only happened once. She doesn't remember it at all. The only problem was my wife caught me in the act. She left me that night. I had to act fast. She was going to ruin my career. So I hired another freak like me to kill her, and I didn't even have to pay him because you killed him. I want to thank you for that. That saved me a little money. Everything kind of snowballed after that. I had to kill the councilman because he was just like me, trying to hide a secret that lived in that scumbag I just killed. He was the last one, although he did have certain talents.

"Smiling Eddie developed a pill. He called them baby roofies and was testing them on the child he stole, Amber Sally. She has no memory of him raping her, under the influence of the drug. He also developed a low-voltage, child-sized Taser; he was a sick genius. He could provide us with young children. They never even knew they were being molested. Thanks to the pills, I stumbled across an easy way to rape someone without them even knowing it.

"And you know what really pisses me off? I liked you. I could see myself marrying you. Then you got smart and figured everything out. Now I have to kill you. Oh well. Edward is going to kill you."

Jamie couldn't believe what she was hearing. She had idolized this man. She kept trying to move, but she could not. The captain knelt down beside her. He grabbed the back of her head and kissed her on the mouth. He told her he didn't want to kill her. "I may have my fetish for young girls, but, baby, you're hot. I was grooming you to be my next wife, and now you have screwed up everything. My perfect plan was to kill him and save you, but now Edward has to kill you, and I will be distraught again."

He dragged Jamie and laid her down beside Edward's body. He pulled a gun out of Edward's pants and placed it in the dead man's hand. He pointed the gun at Jamie.

Sarah was waking up. A bolt of lightning hit a nearby tree and crashed in the street. The wind howled, and the rain poured down. Trashcans were rolling down the street. Little Sarah stood up, staring outside. She shouted, "Mommy, Mommy." She ran out into the street in the pouring rain.

The captain ran to the door and looked outside. His stepdaughter had run to a nearby stop sign and was holding on to it. She kept screaming, "Mommy!" Lightning was striking all around. The captain ran toward his daughter, shouting, "Sally, come inside. You're going to get electrocuted."

At that very instant, a small bolt of lightning hit the stop sign. The sign started glowing, and a face appeared out of the glow—the face of the captain's former wife. The captain was now paralyzed as he stared at the apparition. He started to back up slowly, in fear, as the stop sign rattled in the wind and the rain rocked the sign back and forth. Sarah hung on as her mother's face glowed on the sign. The captain turned and ran back toward the house.

Another bolt of lightning struck the sign. The wind howled as it ripped through the night with the force of hurricane winds. The sign flew through the air like a flying saucer and hit Captain Jackson in the back, knocking him to the ground. He tried to reach the stop sign, which was stuck in his back. He couldn't, so he crawled toward the house.

Amber had gone to Jamie's side. The little girl nudged her. Jamie turned her head slightly toward the little girl and asked her to help her; she was trying to roll toward the front door so she could see what was happening outside. She asked Amber to bring her the gun lying beside the dead man.

Amber placed the gun in Jamie's hand and Jamie squeezed and held it. But she still couldn't lift her arm up. She tried repeatedly but could not. Jamie had heard a high-pitched scream from Sarah outside.

Jamie was trying to see what happened. It couldn't be. *How did that get there?* she asked herself. A stop sign was stuck in Captain Jackson's back. As lightning struck, the rain was pouring down. He crawled toward the house and up the steps. He pulled his weapon out and pointed it at Jamie.

She tried to lift her hand so that she could point her gun and fire at him. But she couldn't.

Just as he was about to pull the trigger, another stop sign crashed down onto his hand. Lightning had struck again at that very instance. He rolled over and pulled another gun out of his jacket.

Jamie looked at the little girl, Amber, and shouted at her, "Help me with my arm!"

Amber helped Jamie lift her arm, pointing it toward the captain as he raised his gun, ready to fire.

Four shots rang out instantaneously. The captain lay motionless on the steps. Jamie had been hit in the shoulder. She had missed Captain Jackson, but lucky for her, Detective Nelson and Officer Garrison had not missed.

Garrison ran to her side. The effects of the Taser had not entirely faded, and she was still more or less paralyzed. "How did you get here?" she asked Officer Garrison. "How did you know?"

"After I text messaged you telling you that I suspected the captain might somehow be involved, I got your message about meeting you at the phone booth outside the donut shop. I immediately called Detective Nelson. I put a bulletproof vest on, and he watched my back, as I expected I'd be shot.

"And Detective Nelson believed my theories. I showed him the printout. I had figured out the code. Kirk stood for captain, Kimball stood for Richard, and Andrew stood for Jackson. I didn't get it until little Sarah had some *Star Trek* movies in her DVD player and a movie, *The Fugitive.* Also, when I put those names into his computer, I had all the evidence I needed to prove he was the killer of the councilman and his wife and the two other people who were killed while we were doing this investigation. It was Captain Richard Jackson. He killed them all, with the help of Edward Grins. If he would have killed me and you when he tried, he would've gotten away with it."

He asked Jamie, "When did you know? When did you figure it out?"

She whispered to him, "He called her Sally. And the other little girl, Amber, had the same exact burn mark on her back that Sarah did. Plus, he loved codes. That's why all the stop signs that said "Stop

Raping Sally" were all spelled SALY—they are initials for Sarah Ann Lavone Young."

Detective Nelson looked at the stop sign stuck in Captain Jackson's back. It had a new message now: "I stopped you!"

Little Sarah had come and sat down beside Jamie. She told Jamie, "My mommy was here. She told me that my daddy was bad. My daddy was the bad man in my dreams who hurt me. She said I should go live with Grandma and Grandpa. Now will you take me?"

The feeling was returning to Jamie's arms and legs. She pulled Sarah toward her and said, "Yes. I will take you!"

Sarah looked into Jamie's eyes and asked, "Will you take me to McDonald's first? I'm hungry!"

"Yes," Jamie said. "Let's all go to McDonald's." She got to her feet, holding on to little Sarah's hand. Sarah had taken Amber's hand.

The trio walked to Jamie's car.

Detective Nelson stopped her. "You can't go," he said. "You've been shot."

She looked at him. "What are you going to do, shoot me?"

She opened her car door, and the two little girls jumped in her car.

Detective Nelson told Officer Garrison to take them to McDonald's and make sure Jamie got to a hospital!

Alternate Ending

"Someone's coming," the captain told Jamie. He moved across the hallway to get a better view of the front door.

Jamie told Amber to sit quietly as she moved into position, trying to see the front door.

A man entered the front door. It was Edward Grins. He shouted out, "Hey, Ritchie. Look what I found." He was dragging a little girl inside the door.

Jamie couldn't see the child, but she looked at the captain. He mouthed the name *Sally*.

Suddenly, three shots rang out. Edward dropped to the ground on top of Sally. In that split second, everything seemed clear to Jamie. She rushed at little Sarah and pulled Edward off of the child. Sarah immediately hugged her. She was crying.

Jamie turned toward Captain Jackson and shouted at him, "It was you. It was you all along." But she made a fatal mistake.

As Captain Jackson dropped his weapon, he said to Jamie, "What are you talking about?"

Jamie felt like a bolt of lightning had struck her in the pit of her back. Then two shots were fired right beside her ear, and Captain Jackson fell to the ground.

Jamie had also fallen to the ground. She was paralyzed. She had been Tasered by Edward Grins. The electrical charge had also paralyzed little Sarah. Jamie tried to move repeatedly but could not.

Edward stood up. He turned Jamie's face toward him and said, "I'd bet you didn't see that coming?" He then pointed at his shirt and pulled it up, revealing a bulletproof vest. He continued to tell Jamie of his conquest. "I just have to tell someone what I did to Captain Jackson." He continued, "This was a setup from the get-go, and it took a lot of planning. Then you screwed it up by killing my friend in that bar that night. So I used you to get him. I wanted him to go on trial for raping his stepdaughter. There is nothing that can ruin your life quicker than child rape, and believe me, I know.

"Twenty years ago, Richard Jackson was a rookie cop dating my sister. I was thirteen years old at the time. One night, I was babysitting the next-door neighbor's kid. Your captain and my sister walked in while I was playing a harmless game of show-and-tell. The next thing I knew, I was put into reform school and charged with child molestation. He ruined my life and turned me into the sick fuck I am now, so I drugged him and raped his daughter. I tried one of my new drugs on her so she would remember a little bit. I even jacked him off so I could leave some of his semen on her. I left him lying there beside her.

"His wife came home. It was perfect. I put the kiddie porn sites on his computer. My friend was going to kill his wife and testify that he paid him to do it to cover up the rape of their stepdaughter, and you had to kill him." He kicked Jamie as she lay on the floor. "So I had to scramble to plan B. I left you all these simple clues, all pointing to Captain Jackson. I even left you messages from his dying wife: 'Stop Raping Sally.' How clever that was of me. I knew that her mother called her Sally because of her initials and that

Captain Jackson was trying to get her to be called Sarah, her real name, because she became sad when someone called her Sally. Isn't that sweet?

"And all I have to do to finish things off in one perfect package is put my gun in your hand and fire one more shot in Captain Richard Jackson." It was now raining hard.

Thunder and lightning filled the night sky, and the wind was really blowing. Suddenly, the front door blew open. Edward pried Jamie and Sarah apart and dragged Jamie over toward the captain's body. He placed the gun in her hand. A huge lightning strike had hit a nearby tree and exploded.

Sarah was white as she rubbed her eyes. She looked out into the stormy night. She started screaming, "Mommy, Mommy, I'm coming."

She ran out into the storm toward a nearby stop sign. She clutched the sign like it was her mother's leg.

Edward ran after her, his gun trained on the child. "Come here, child," he said. "Come to me. You're going to get electrocuted."

Then the sign started glowing. A face appeared in the sign. Edward looked on in horror. It was Sally's mother's face. He started walking backward; then he turned and ran, turning back to fire a couple of shots at the sign.

In the blink of an eye, lightning struck the sign. The wind picked up, hurling the stop sign into Edward's back and knocking him to the ground. He reached back behind him and could feel the sign poking out of his back. He started crawling toward the house

Inside, Jamie felt some brief movement. She was trying to pull her gun out of its holster, but her fingers and hands were still not working right. The other little girl had come out of the back room. Jamie told her to come and help her. The little girl pulled Jamie's gun from her holster and put it in Jamie's hand, but Jamie could not lift her arm.

The little girl lifted Jamie's arm and pointed her arm at the front door. Edward crawled through the front door, got to his knees, and pointed his gun at Jamie. Jamie tried to fire. She squeezed with all her might, hoping her finger would respond to her command. Two shots rang out simultaneously.

Edward Grins was dead, and Captain Richard Jackson fell beside Jamie. He had gotten to his feet and fired one last shot. With his dying breath, he told Jamie to make sure Sarah was placed with her grandparents. That's what his wife would have wanted.

Jamie could hear police sirens coming in the background. It was over. She watched a man who she cared about, a man she could have seen a future with—and who she just accused of terrible things—die in front of his child. She felt so much compassion and pain for his child. She felt very stupid at this moment. He was a good father!